UGLY BUGS
AND
NASTY NATURE

Two Horrible Books in One

NICK ARNOLD
TONY DE SAULLES

■ SCHOLASTIC

Scholastic Children's Books,
Euston House, 24 Eversholt Street, London NW1 1DB, UK

A division of Scholastic Ltd
London ~ New York ~ Toronto ~ Sydney ~ Auckland
Mexico City ~ New Delhi ~ Hong Kong

Published in this edition by Scholastic Ltd, 2005
Cover illustration copyright © Tony De Saulles, 2005

Ugly Bugs
First published in the UK by Scholastic Ltd, 1996
Text copyright © Nick Arnold, 1996
Illustrations copyright © Tony De Saulles, 1996

Nasty Nature
First published in the UK by Scholastic Ltd, 1997
Text copyright © Nick Arnold, 1997
Illustrations copyright © Tony De Saulles, 1997

10 digit ISBN 0 439 95454 1
13 digit ISBN 978 0439 95454 9

Printed and bound by Nørhaven Paperback A/S, Denmark

10 9 8 7 6 5 4 3 2

The right of Nick Arnold and Tony De Saulles to be identified as the author and
illustrator of this work respectively has been asserted by them in accordance
with the Copyright, Designs and Patents Act, 1988.

Papers used by Scholastic Children's Books are made from wood
grown in sustainable forests.

Contents

Ugly Bugs

Introduction	7
Ugly bug families	9
Weird worms	20
Slimy snails and ugly slugs	31
Underwater uglies	37
Creepy-crawlies	45
Insect invaders	55
Horrible beetles	63
Awesome ants	71
Sleazy bees	80
Pretty uglies	85
Savage spiders	94
Biting bugs	105
Devious disguises	115
Ugly bugs vs horrible humans	121

Nasty Nature

Introduction	133
Freaky creatures	135
Dumb animals?	152
Snarls, growls and howls	167

Terrible travels   182
Nice and nasty: helpers and hangers on   193
Horrible hunters   206
Poisoned prey   224
Narrow squeaks   233
Gruesome guzzling   246
A bit of breeding   264
Nocturnal nasties   277
Nasty nature?   286

UGLY BUGS

Nick Arnold has been writing stories and books since he was a youngster, but never dreamt he'd find fame writing about Horrible Science. His research involved being stung, cuddling up to snakes and being covered with slime and he enjoyed every minute of it.

When he's not delving into Horrible Science, Nick spends (almost!) all his time writing. If he's got a spare moment, his hobbies include eating pizza, riding his bike and thinking up corny jokes (though not all at the same time).

Tony De Saulles picked up his crayons when he was still in nappies and has been doodling ever since. He takes Horrible Science very seriously and even agreed to investigate what happens when you make friends with poisonous ants and hungry lions. Fortunately, he has made a full recovery.

When he's not out with his sketchpad, Tony likes to write poetry and play squash, though he hasn't written any poetry about squash yet.

Introduction

Science can be horribly mysterious. Not just science homework – it's a mystery how they expect you to do it all. No, I mean – science itself. For example, what do scientists do all day? Ask a scientist and you'll just get a load of scientific jargon.

I STUDY BIO-LUMINESCENCE IN COLEOPTERA*

*ENGLISH TRANSLATION. I'M LOOKING AT BEETLES THAT GLOW IN THE DARK.

It all sounds horribly confusing. And horribly boring. But it shouldn't be. You see, science isn't about all-knowing experts in white coats and laboratories and hi-tech gadgetry. Science is about **us**. How we live and what happens to us every day.

And the best bits of science are also the most horrible bits. That's what this book is about. Not science, but **horrible** science. Take ugly bugs for instance. You don't need to go very far to find them. Lift up any stone and something crawls out. Look into any dark, creepy corner and there's some ugly bug lurking there. Decide on a nice early morning bath and you might discover you'll be sharing it with a huge hairy spider.

You see, ugly bugs bring science to life. Horrible life. Especially when you find out how a praying mantis catches its victims – and bites their heads off. Here's your chance to find out many more truly horrible facts about ugly bugs. And discover why for some ignorant adults an ugly bug – any ugly bug – is something to be swatted or sprayed out of existence.

Mind you, it's a good idea to keep this book out of reach of grown-ups because:

1 They might want to read it too.

2 It might give them bad dreams.

3 When you've read it you'll be far better informed than they are. You can tell them a few horrible but true scientific facts. And science will never seem the same again.

Ugly bug families

The worst thing about ugly bugs is that there are so many of them. There are thousands and thousands of different types. They have to be sorted out before we can even begin to get to know them. It's a horrible job – but someone has to do it. Don't worry, though, it won't be you – here's a list some scientists prepared earlier.

Each type of living thing is called a species and these species are put into larger groups called genera a bit like belonging to a club. Groups of genera make families. Confused yet? You will be.

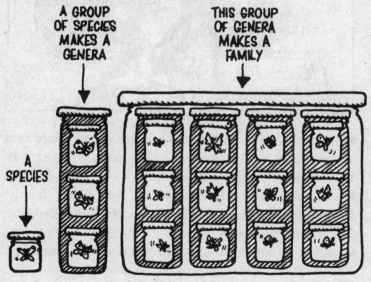

A GROUP OF SPECIES MAKES A GENERA

THIS GROUP OF GENERA MAKES A FAMILY

A SPECIES

Like any family, ugly bug family members look a bit alike. But they don't all live together in a neat little home. If they did they might start fighting over who uses the bathroom first in the morning.

Groups of related families are known as "orders". And scientists lump orders together to make huge groups called "classes". (This is nothing to do with school, even if the classes have to follow orders.)

Here's an example of what we're talking about. This little bug is a seven-spot ladybird.

MAKES ME SOUND LIKE AN ITALIAN ICE-CREAM!

Coccinella septum punctata

- Its scientific name is *Coccinella septum punctata* (try saying that with a mouthful of popcorn) – which is Latin for . . . seven-spot ladybird.
- And ladybirds belong to an ugly bug family called *Coccinellidae* (cock-in-ell-id-day), or ladybirds. (Surprise, surprise!)
- Ladybirds belong to the order *Coleoptera* (coe-le-op-ter-ra), that's beetles to you.
- Beetles belong to the class *Insecta,* or insects.

Simple, really! And it makes good sense for ugly bugs to be organised. There are more than 350,000 species of beetle alone. Try sorting that lot into matchboxes! So, now you know how the system works, why not flip through the ugly bug family album? First let's meet some . . .

Irritating Insects

Insect bodies are divided into three parts – a head, a middle bit or thorax and a bit at the back called an abdomen. An insect has two feelers (antennae) on its head and three pairs of legs attached to its thorax. Scientists have identified about a million insect species with bodies like these and there are plenty more just waiting to be discovered.

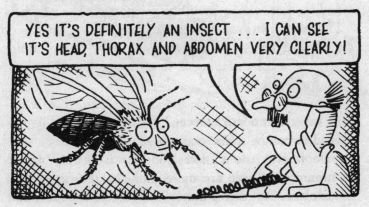

Earwigs 1,000 species. Earwigs get their name from the barmy belief that they crawl into your ears when you're asleep! They have mean-looking pincers at the back of their bodies. Males have curved pincers and females have straight ones.

Grasshoppers, crickets and locusts 20,000 species. They jump around and produce noises by rubbing their legs together to make themselves irresistible to the opposite sex.

Stick insects and leaf insects 2,000 species. Most live in tropical forests. Stick insects are so called because, well, they look like sticks, and leaf insects are so called because, you guessed it, they look like leaves. Either way they sit about all day looking like part of the furniture.

Know anyone like that? It's a clever disguise, of course, but what a life!

Beetles At least 350,000 species in this order worldwide – that's more than any other type of animal. But you'd never be able to catch them all in a jam jar. Apart from their vast numbers, many of them are known only as a single example in a museum collection.

Termites 2,000 species. Termites like a nice hot climate. They are small soft insects but that doesn't mean they're a soft touch. Termites build nests that look like palaces and are ruled by kings and queens. Guard-termites are so serious about their work they sometimes explode in a bid to defend the nest!

Ants, bees and wasps 100,000 species in this order worldwide. All members have a narrow waist between the thorax and the abdomen. Most have wings. (Worker ants don't develop wings – they're far too busy to go anywhere.)

Mantids and cockroaches 5,000 species. There's a strong family resemblance in their horrible habits. Cockroaches make midnight raids on the pantry. The praying mantis sits around cunningly disguised as part of a plant, and waits to pounce on its innocent victims.

Bugs 55,000 species in this order worldwide. They suck vegetable juices through straw-like mouths. Nothing ugly about that, you might think, except some do like a bit of blood now and then.

Flies 70,000 species in this order. They use one pair of wings for flying (which is what they do best). They also have the remnants of a second pair of wings, that look like tiny drumsticks, and are actually used for balancing. Most Irritating Fly Habit: flying backwards, sideways and forwards round your head. OK – so you know they're incredible fliers already. Nastiest Fly Habit: some types of fly like nothing better than to lick the top of a big smelly cowpat. And then pay a visit to whatever you were going to have for tea.

Sucking lice 250 species. Lice don't build their own homes. No. They live on other creatures. It's nice and warm there and you can suck a refreshing drop of blood whenever you feel like it. Lice live on all mammals except bats. Or at least no-one has ever found a louse on a bat.

Dragon flies, caddis flies, mayflies are three different orders totalling 9,000 species. They start off living in water and then take to the air. Traditional names for dragon flies include "horse stingers" and "devil's darning needles". Which is odd because they don't sting horses and you can't mend your socks with them.

MAYFLY   CADDISFLY   DRAGONFLY

I DON'T LOOK LIKE A DRAGON EITHER!

Butterflies and moths 165,000 species in this order world-wide. They have two pairs of wings and their young start off as caterpillars. Then they hide in a case called a chrysalis and re-arrange their body parts before emerging as butterflies or moths. It's a bit like you spending a few weeks taking your body apart in a sleeping bag. And then putting it all back together in a different order.

YOU'LL NEVER GET ME UP IN ONE OF THEM!

So these are the ugly insects, but what about their even more repulsive relatives?

Nasty Non-Insects

If an ugly bug has got more than six legs – or no legs at all, it isn't an insect.

Slugs and snails 70,000 species. Many live in the sea. Slimy slugs and snails belong to a huge group of animals called the molluscs that even includes octopuses. But slugs and snails are the only members of the group that have tentacles on their heads.

Centipedes and millipedes are two different classes of ugly bugs. There are about 2,800 species of centipede and 6,500 species of millipede. But sinister centipedes gobble up the poor little millipedes and *not* the other way round.

Wood lice Over 2,000 species. They all have seven pairs of legs. Woodlice, would you believe it, belong to the same class of creature as crabs and lobsters!

Spiders There are 35,000 species in this order but scientists think there may be up to five times that number waiting to be discovered! What a thought! Most spiders spin silken webs. They have eight legs, of course and their bodies are divided into two parts.

MONEY SPIDER   TARANTULA SPIDER

Earthworms, bristleworms and leeches 6,800 species altogether. Leeches are the nasty bloodsuckers. When a leech sucks blood it can swell up to three times its original size. There are 300 different leech species. Yuck! One is enough!

Mites There are 20,000 species in this order. Unlike spiders, mites have a one-piece body. Many mites are under 1mm long but they still have some hugely horrible habits. Some eat cheese rinds and the glue in old books. Others suck blood from animals.

So there you have it. Ugly bug families *are* horribly confusing. There are so many of them and they come in a horrible array of shapes and sizes. But they've got one vital feature in common – they're HUNGRY! Take the worms, for example, they like nothing better than a breakfast of slimy rotting leaves. And some worms have even more revolting tastes.

You can't get away from worms. They live in soil. Bet you didn't know their slimy relatives also live in the sea? You might also find them at the bottom of ponds and even inside other creatures. There are thousands of worm species with all sorts of ugly habits. But one thing they all have in common is that they're horribly *weird*.

A disgusting discovery

The Pacific Ocean off the Galapagos Islands, 1977

There was definitely something down there. Something strange and terrifying. Instruments trailing from the research ship far into the depths below revealed strange rises in sea temperature. Cameras lowered into the deep-sea darkness had taken pictures of strange shapes. And water samples taken from the deep stank enough to make you sick. The scientists needed to know more. Someone had to visit those remote depths where no human had ever gone before. But what would they find when they got there?

Metre by metre the submersible slipped ever deeper into the unknown. From the observation window the scientists could make out nothing but the pitch-black freezing cold sea. The surface of the Pacific Ocean was a terrifying 2.5 km (1½ miles) above their heads. And on every square centimetre of the submersible, a tonne of ocean pressed down. In the lights of the tiny craft the scientists could see strange volcanic rocks. But no sign of life. They shivered. Nothing could live down here in this horrible place surely? Then it happened.

The submersible's temperature gauge spun off the scale with a gigantic heat surge. The water turned from black to cloudy blue. The scientists had found a natural chimney that led deep beneath the earth's surface. Here, heated chemicals, stinking like rotten eggs, boil up from below at terrifically high temperatures.

And the hot cloudy water was alive with bacteria too small for the eye to see. The billions of bacteria billowed in vast clouds. Strange ghostly pale crabs scurried through the ooze on the sea bed in search of bits of drowned sea creatures. And there were thousands of giant clams. Then out of the darkness and confusion, the THINGS appeared.

The scientists were astounded. What were these creatures? Were they alien life-forms? Why did they look so weird? The strange red tips of the creatures waved in the sea. Their bodies were hidden in long white upright tubes, each 4 metres (4½ yards) long, and they had red blood just like humans. They were giant seaworms – the largest ever seen and of a type unknown to science. But these ugly bugs had no mouths and no stomachs. So how and what did they eat?

There was only one way to find out. The robot arm of the submersible reached out and grabbed a worm from its strange home. Back on the ship a fearless scientist sliced it open. What do you think he found inside?

a) crabs

b) bits of dead animal that had floated down from the surface.

c) beastly bacteria

Answer: c) A slimy mass of billions of bacteria. The same disgusting chemical-guzzling bacteria that made the water cloudy. But here comes the surprise. The worms weren't actually *eating* the bacteria! Inside the worm's guts, the bacteria ate the smelly chemicals in the water and made new chemicals that the worms could feed off. Quite a cosy arrangement really.

Weird worm varieties

There are three main orders of worms. Flatworms, ribbon worms and segmented worms. So how can you tell which is which?

Weird Flatworms

Surprisingly enough, flatworms get their name because they are pretty flat. Their bodies aren't divided into segments, and they're pretty slimy, too. They're probably the slimiest worm you'll come across.

For example, one type of flatworm, the parasitic tapeworm, can live inside an animal's stomach! Another, called dugeasia, (dug-easi-er) picks on creatures smaller than itself and sucks them up. But if the tiddlers get a bit too big, ugly Dug wraps them up in a slimy parcel and just sucks bits off them.

PARASITIC TAPEWORM

Then there's the milky-white flatworm, a close relative of dugeasia. It lives in water and it's almost see-through, so you can see what it ate for dinner. And when it wants to reproduce it sometimes tears itself in two!

Weird Ribbonworms

Most ribbonworms live in the sea. Sometimes they have weird tube-like structures that shoot out from their heads to catch other unsuspecting worms and smaller creatures.

Ribbonworms can be horribly long. The bootlace worm sometimes reaches several metres. Would you like to meet a worm that's as long as your bootlace?

IMPRESSED?

Weird Segmented Worms

The weird worms in this gruesome group all have rounded bodies that divide into segments. Some of them are parasites, and can cause disease. Others might live in the soil, in the sea, or freshwater. They live on small plants and animals.

Bristleworms belong to this order. Maybe you've spotted them at the seaside? Some of them build tubes out of the sand and sit in them with their tentacles poking out. But uglier bristleworms crawl about looking for prey. They use their two pairs of jaws, two pairs of feelers and four tentacles to search out their food. They particularly enjoy sucking the insides out of snails. Yummy!

A sea mouse, on the other hand has a mouse-shaped body that's all furry. Aahh, sounds quite cute, doesn't it? Except that this worm can grow up to 18 cm (7 inches) long, and 7 cm (3 inches) wide. Sounds more like a sea rat!

Want to get friendly with a member of the segmented worm family? Then let's get . . .

Down-to-earthworms

Fearsome fact file

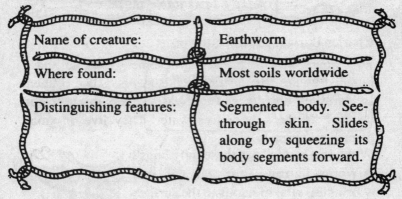

Name of creature:	Earthworm
Where found:	Most soils worldwide
Distinguishing features:	Segmented body. See-through skin. Slides along by squeezing its body segments forward.

Visual identification

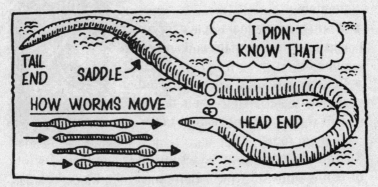

Are earthworms awful?
"Yes", according to people who don't like slimy wriggling creatures.

"No", according to some very famous naturalists. Gilbert White wrote in 1770 . . . .

Earthworms though in appearance a small and despicable link in the Chain of Nature, yet if lost would make a lamentable chasm.

Charles Darwin called earthworms . . .

Earthworms have played a most important part in the history of the world.

What's so great about these ugly bugs?

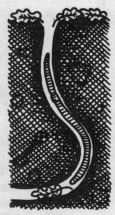

- Worm burrows mix up the soil bringing vital minerals to the surface so hungry plants can easily slurp them up.
- Worm burrows make space for water and air to mix with the soil and reach plant roots.
- Earthworms drag leaves and other rotting material into their burrows. This rotting material can be taken up by plant roots.

So you see crops grow better in soil where there are lots of earthworms. In fact in Europe and the USA there are earthworm farms that produce up to 500,000 worms a day for sale to farmers. Good old earthworms!

But earthworms are still ugly bugs, so they do have

some horrible habits. After the earth has passed through their bodies it ends up in ugly earthworm shaped piles all over your beautiful front lawn. Earthworms love to guzzle lettuce and their burrowing can damage plant seedlings. Never mind – if your earthworms turn nasty you can always use them as fishing bait.

Are you an earthworm expert?

You may think that earthworms are deadly dull and boring. And of course, you'd be right. But delve a little deeper into their humdrum lives and you'll discover some slimy surprises. See if you can guess these answers.

1 How many worms could you count per hectare (2½ acres) of farmland?

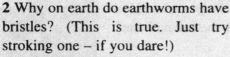

a) Three
b) 65,697
c) Two million

2 Why on earth do earthworms have bristles? (This is true. Just try stroking one – if you dare!)
a) To help them move along.
b) To stop the early bird from yanking them out of the soil.
c) To sweep their burrows clean.

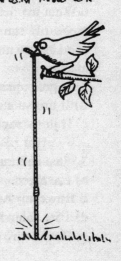

3 How on earth does a worm accidentally bury a stone?
a) The stone rolls into a hole dug by the worm to catch beetles.

b) Worms push earth up from their burrows until the stone is covered.
c) Worms tunnel under the stone. The stone falls into the tunnel.

4 How long was the longest earthworm ever found?
a) 20 cm (8 inches)
b) 45.5 cm (18 inches)
c) 6.7 metres (22 feet)

5 Worms have a part of their body called a saddle. What on earth is it used for?
a) To give rides to earwigs.
b) To carry lumps of food.
c) To carry eggs about.

6 What happens when you cut a short piece off the end of a worm? (No need to try this out to discover the answer.)
a) It gets upset.
b) It grows a new tail.
c) It joins back together again.

7 What on earth do moles do to worms?
a) Eat them.
b Bite their heads off.
c) Bite their heads off *and* let them escape.

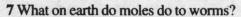

Answers: 1 c) Amazingly enough. **2 a)** *and* **b)**! Trick question, sorry. **3 b)** This makes the soil level rise and things level with the soil sink down. **4 c)** It was a type of giant earthworm that lives in South Africa. This monster wriggled out of the ground in Transvaal in 1937. **5 c)** The saddle is a belt that moves the length of the worm picking up the fertilised eggs. The worm wriggles free leaving the eggs in a cocoon. **6 b). 7** Another trick question. The answer is all three! **a)** Moles love a juicy earthworm. **b)** When they're full they bite their heads off and put them in their "pantry". This doesn't kill the worms it just stops them escaping! **c)** But sometimes a worm has time to grow another head and escape!

How to charm a worm

What you need

a fine day, but not too dry

a lawn or flowerbed (make sure the soil is slightly damp)

a pitchfork (optional)

a hi-fi speaker (optional)

What to do

1 You are going to pretend to be rain.

2 You can make vibrations by jumping up and down, playing music with the speaker facing the ground,

or by sticking a pitchfork into the ground and wiggling it about a lot (this is also known as "twanging"). Alternatively, use your imagination to create your own short, sharp shower.

But why does this make the worms come out?

Worms like rain because they have to keep their skin moist to prevent it drying out. When they feel the rain drops hitting the ground they pop their heads out to take a look.

Bet you never knew

You can "charm" an earthworm. Every summer a primary school in Nantwich, England hosts a weird competition. It's the world worm charming championship. Yes – it's true. What a charming traditional pastime!

Slimy snails and ugly slugs

They're covered in slime, slide along very slowly and have eyes on the end of stalks. And if that's not ugly enough, they gobble up your garden lettuce. So it's not surprising that people don't like them. But are slugs and snails really that horrible? Do they deserve their rotten reputation? Yes they do. And here's why.

Fearsome fact file

Name of creatures:	Slugs and snails
Where found:	Worldwide in the soil, in the sea and in fresh water. Land slugs and snails like damp places.
Distinguishing features:	Snails have shells on their backs. Slugs don't.

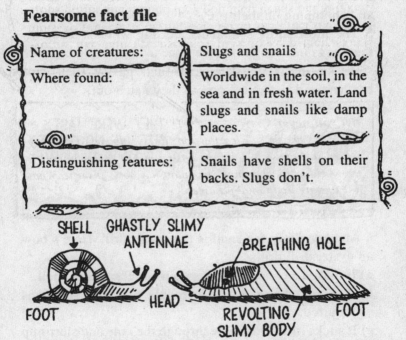

SHELL GHASTLY SLIMY ANTENNAE BREATHING HOLE
FOOT HEAD REVOLTING SLIMY BODY FOOT

Seven slimy snail facts you didn't really want to know

1 The largest snail in the world is the African Giant snail. It can be 34 cm (13 inches) from its shell top to its head!

It eats bananas – and dead animals.

2 The garlic grass snail smells strongly of garlic. OK – it's not really horrible. But it must give snail-eating birds horribly bad breath.

3 When a snail is chomping away on your mum's prize cauliflowers, it will be using its radula – that's its tongue. The radula is so rough it actually grates its food.

4 Some sea snails on the other hand, eat meat. These snails have a few sharp teeth – well suited for catching and chomping on their prey!

5 The most slimy sea snails are dog whelks. They lay their eggs in a tough capsule attached to the sea bed. But some of the youngsters seize and guzzle their own brothers and sisters as soon as they hatch out!

THEY WERE TASTY – BUT I'VE NO ONE TO PLAY WITH NOW!

6 Another slimy sea snail is the oyster drill. Here's how an oyster drill drills:

a) It makes a chemical that softens up the oyster shell.

b) It scrapes the shell with its radula, repeating step **a)** as required.

c) It sticks its feeding tube through the hole and slurps up the juicy oyster!

7 But snails don't have it all their own way. A tiny worm lives inside the amber snail. Sometimes the worm releases chemicals that turn the snail's tentacles orange!

This colourful display attracts a bird that nips off the snail's crowning glory. The worm begins a whole gruesome new life inside the bird. And the snail? It grows new tentacles. So that's all right then.

Ugly slugs

A slug is just a slimy snail without a mobile home on its back. Come to think of it – slugs have the right idea. Have you ever seen a snail trying to get under a really low bridge? Not having a shell helps the slug to slither into nooks and crannies. But slugs have some scintillating secrets. That's if you dare discover them.

Dare YOU make friends with . . . an ugly slug?

Here's how to snuggle up to a slug. Who knows, you could be in for a horribly interesting encounter!

1 First meet your slug. You can tell where there are slugs around by the horrible silvery slime trails they leave. They like to slither about in the open on warm damp summer evenings. So just follow a tempting trail until you find your slug lurking under the leaves of a small plant.

2 Enjoy that gooey, squelchy feel between your fingers as you put your slug in a glass jar.

3 Watch in amazement as your ugly slug climbs the slippery walls of the jar. It moves on a layer of slime produced by its foot. The sticky slime allows the slug to cling to the glass. Waves of movement push its foot forward. Think about it – could you climb up a glass wall on just one foot that's been dipped in something rather like raw egg?

4 Imagine you were a bird. Would you want to eat the slug? Not likely – the slime tastes disgusting! But hedgehogs think they are horribly delicious.

5 Put your new friend back where you found him/her. That way you'll stay friends.

If you go slug hunting in your garden on a warm damp night you might meet a shield-shelled slug. (Try saying that very fast – three times!) This sinister slug gets its name from a tiny shell on the top end of its body. But can you guess what it eats? Clue: It isn't lettuce.

Answer: Earthworms, centipedes and other slugs. Delicious!

Seven ugly slug facts

1 The largest British ugly slug is the great grey slug. It grows to 20 cm (8 inches) long!

2 But that's nothing! Some sea slugs are 40 cm (16 inches) long and weigh 7 kilos (15 pounds). They are also often brightly coloured.

3 And some of them have some horribly strange habits. Glaucus is a sea slug that floats upside-down buoyed up by an air bubble inside its stomach.

4 Meanwhile back on the farm, slugs and farmers are sworn enemies because ugly slugs eat or spoil crops. If slugs didn't eat potatoes there would be enough extra chips to feed 400,000 people for a year!

5 And land slugs have some horribly strange habits as well. Some ugly slugs can let themselves down from a height on a string of slime.

6 Like worms and snails, slugs are both male and female at the same time.

7 When slugs mate they cling together and cover themselves in slime. Then they fire little arrows called love darts at one another to get in the mood. Very romantic – if you're a slug!

Bet you never knew
An ugly slug can tell you which way the wind is blowing. It's true. A slug will always crawl away from the prevailing wind. Slugs do this to stop themselves drying out too quickly.

Underwater uglies

Why not relax by a peaceful pond or river and forget about horrible ugly bugs? Some chance! Ugly bugs like water even more than you do. And those murky waters hide some pretty ugly undercurrents.

WINTER ~freezing.
Ugly bugs have to hide in the mud at the bottom.

SPRING ~rain.
Acid rain is very bad for ugly bugs.

SUMMER ~warm and sunny.
If the weather gets too hot the pond will dry up!

AUTUMN ~soggy.
Leaves can clog the pond. As they rot they use up all the oxygen and the ugly bugs die!

Imagine a pond as a kind of living soup. It's full of tiny plants and animals. The largest animals are always trying to eat the smaller ones, and the smaller animals are trying to eat even smaller animals, and they're all trying not to be eaten by each other. Scientists call this a food web because you get in a tangle if you try to figure out who eats who.

A pond is a perilous place to live. And its not just other animals bugs have to watch out for. There are plenty of hazards all year round.

And at all times, horrible humans chuck in harmful rubbish and poisonous pollution. And then they drain the pond!

Ugly underwater lifestyles

Every freshwater ugly bug has developed its own methods of living and eating. See if you can match each ugly bug to its loathsome lifestyle?

1 Hangs under the water surface and breathes through a tube. Grabs a passing bug in its claws and sucks out the juices.

2 Lives in an underwater diving bell made from silk and air bubbles. Eats anything that moves.

3 Hangs upside-down from the surface and stores air in its shell. Eats tiny plants.

4 Walks around on the surface looking for bugs that have fallen in. Its light body and widely spaced legs ensure it doesn't break the water tension. (That's the springy top surface of the water.)

5 Lives in the water and leaps to escape. Lives off tiny plants.

6 Swims round in circles on the surface and dives to escape danger. Has four eyes – one pair of eyes above the water and one pair below. It can also fly! Eats other pond bugs.

a) WATER SCORPION

b) WATER MEASURER

c) WHIRLIGIG BEETLE

d) GREAT POND SNAIL

e) WATER FLEA

f) WATER SPIDER

Answers: 1 a) 2 f) 3 d) 4 b) 5 e) 6 c)

39

Ugly water sports

As long as conditions in the pond are right and there is plenty of food, life for a pond ugly bug must seem one long holiday. Is this a holiday you could do without?

WELCOME TO UGLY BUG WATER WORLD!

The water sports centre where leisure is lethal!

The small print.
We can't guarantee your safety.
If you get eaten it's not our fault ~ Okay?

A Great Dive!

Dive into danger with the great diving beetle. Store air bubbles under your wings to stay down for longer. Also learn to grab and guzzle any underwater edibles.

Rafting & fishing

Enjoy a lazy paddle with our resident raft spider. As you float by on your leaf raft try a spot of fishing. Just dip one of your eight legs in the water to attract little fish.

I THINK WE'LL STAY AT HOME THIS YEAR KIDS!

 # Power Beetle Boat racing

Race a rove beetle boat. Hang on tight as the boating beetle bombs across the water. All our beetles feature the latest jet-propelled abdomen gas engines.

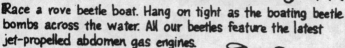

Water good swim!

Learn basic backstroke with our brilliant backswimming water boatman beetle. Swimming on your front lesson taught by his assistant - the lesser water boatman.

Now you've worked up an appetite. Where better to relax than our exclusive underwater eating places?

The Caddis Fly Larva Cafe

Gravel built with silk wallpaper - it's the perfect place for a relaxing and informal meal. Book now before your caddis fly chef grows up and flies away. Vegetarian? Don't worry! The nearby Veggie Caddis Fly Cafe offers a choice of tiny slimy plants and bits of rotting leaves. <u>Warning to patrons. Beware the treacherous trout. They sometimes try to eat the cafe.</u>

Café

BEWARE OF THE TROUT!

Bet you never knew!

May or June is when mayflies hatch out and have the day of their lives. Literally. They only live a day or so. They mate, lay their eggs and die. Ugly bugs and fearsome fish go crazy banqueting on the bodies.

HAPPY BIRTHDAY!

Loathsome leeches

Lurking at the bottom of your local pond or canal is a creature that makes the others seem quite likeable. There's no way of disguising it. These creatures are *loathsome*!

Ugly bug fact file

Name of creature:	Leech
Where found:	Worldwide in water or damp rain forests.
Horrible habits:	Sucks blood
Any helpful habits:	Used in medicine to . . . suck blood (surprisingly enough)!
Distinguishing features:	Long segmented body with suckers at the back and front.

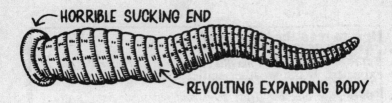

← HORRIBLE SUCKING END

REVOLTING EXPANDING BODY

The most loathsome leech awards

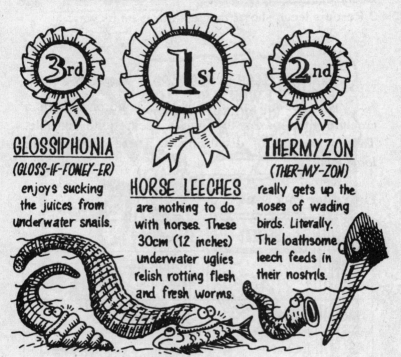

GLOSSIPHONIA
(GLOSS-IF-FONEY-ER)
enjoys sucking
the juices from
underwater snails.

HORSE LEECHES
are nothing to do
with horses. These
30cm (12 inches)
underwater uglies
relish rotting flesh
and fresh worms.

THERMYZON
(THER-MY-ZON)
really gets up the
noses of wading
birds. Literally.
The loathsome
leech feeds in
their nostrils.

A loathsome leech barometer

But even leeches have their uses. Here is a vile Victorian invention it's best *not* to try. Simply place a leech in a jar of fresh pond water. Cover the top of the jar with a fine cloth and secure tightly. Feed your barometer on blood now and then.

How to read the barometer

1 Leech climbs to the top of the jar means that rain is expected. If the weather settles down again, so will the leech.

2 Lazy leech lies on the bottom of its jar means fine or frosty weather.

3 Restless leech shows that a storm is on its way.

Creepy-crawlies

Who hasn't looked under a stone at one time or another and seen an assortment of horrible-looking creatures? Chances are that these creepy-crawlies included centipedes, millipedes and woodlice. Now you might think that because these creatures live in the same place they'd all be mates. Well, you'd be horribly wrong. Centipedes like to eat millipedes – when they get the chance. And that's just the start of their disgusting differences!

Ugly bug fact file

Name of creatures:	Centipedes and millipedes
Where found:	Worldwide, often amongst leaf litter and rotten wood.
Distinguishing features:	Centipede: Segmented, slightly flattened body. Two jointed legs on each segment; two long feelers. Millipede: Segmented, rounded body. Four jointed legs on each segment; two short feelers.

ANTENNAE

HEAD

CENTIPEDE

MILLIPEDE

Creepy comparisons

1 Feet count Millipede means "thousand feet" – which just goes to show that some scientists can't count. Millipedes never have more than 300 feet.

Centipede means "hundred feet". But once again the scientists got it horribly wrong! Many centipedes have fewer than 30 feet.

2 Walking When a millipede walks, waves of movement pass up its body so that it glides along. When a centipede walks it raises alternate legs just as you normally do. It has extra long legs at the back so it doesn't trip up.

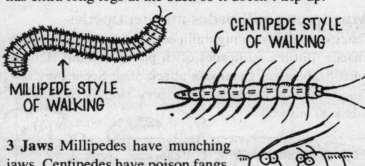

MILLIPEDE STYLE OF WALKING

CENTIPEDE STYLE OF WALKING

3 Jaws Millipedes have munching jaws. Centipedes have poison fangs. They're both pretty ugly.

4 Romantic problems Millipedes have a big problem – they can't see very well. So male millipedes have developed some strange ways of attracting a mate.

● Some bang their heads on the ground.
● Others let out a loud screech.
● Some produce special scents.
● Others rub their legs together to make sounds.

A male centipede, on the other hand, has other things on his mind. All centipedes are horribly aggressive and the female he fancies is quite capable of eating him! So first of all he walks around her, tapping her with his feelers to show he's friendly.

Murderous millipedes and centipedes

Centipedes enjoy eating millipedes – when they get the chance. But the millipedes often put up a fight! Here's what happens. . . Centipede attack plan: Spear prey on fangs and inject poison. Once prey stops wriggling – nibble at leisure.

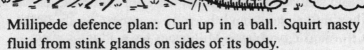

Millipede defence plan: Curl up in a ball. Squirt nasty fluid from stink glands on sides of its body.

Who do you think has the best chance of winning – the menacing millipedes or the sinister centipedes?

In some parts of the world, centipedes and millipedes can grow to gigantic proportions. Giant millipedes can measure up to 26 cm (10 inches) long.

Some of these monsters have fearsome fangs. One type of centipede in the Solomon Islands has a particularly painful bite. People have been known to plunge their hands into *boiling water* to take their minds off the pain! In Malaysia the local centipede's bite has been described by travellers as worse than a snake's. And in India there are even scarier stories of people who were *killed* by giant centipede bites.

Mind you, the millipedes aren't much better. In Haiti in the West Indies giant millipedes attack the local chickens and sometimes blind them with jets of poison! Other giant millipedes produce little puffs of poison gas. The gas kills any attacking animal.

CHICKEN TONIGHT!

But size doesn't save either the giant centipedes or the giant millipedes from a horribly gruesome death. In the African savannah giant hornbills are often seen plodding along looking at the ground. Suddenly they will nab a passing centipede in their long beak, and the centipede has no chance to bite the bird back. Scrunch, crunch, gobble and poor old deadly giant centipede has turned into another scrumptious snack for the hornbill.

Other centipedes get carried away by armies of ants. OK, the centipede can easily kill a few hundred ants but when it's 10,000 ants to one centipede, the poor old centipede doesn't stand a chance!

Giant millipedes have it tough too. Grey meerkats often feed on millipedes. Funny thing is that the meerkats always screw their faces up in disgust when they're eating. Well, who would expect a millipede to taste good?

Dare YOU make friends with . . . a millipede?

Now for the good news. In this country millipedes are quite harmless. Just as long as you handle them gently – and as long as you don't try to make a meal of them. Here's how to make a meal *for* them instead, just to show what a good pal you are.

1 First catch your millipede. (And make sure it *is* a millipede, *not* a centipede!) Millipede's lurk in shady places, so try looking under leaf litter, compost or loose tree bark.

2 Pop your new friend into a small jar partly filled with earth – and a piece of a bark so it can hide.

3 Then serve up a tasty treat. A millipede's mouth would water at the thought of a ripe raspberry, a piece of potato skin, a mouldy old lettuce leaf or a little chunk of apple.

4 Place the jar in a dark secluded place.

5 Next day find out which delicious dish the millipede preferred.

6 Then it's time to say good-bye to your millipede mate. So pop your guest back where you found it. There is sure to be plenty of food and shelter there and let's hope there are no centipedes loitering nearby. Otherwise your millipede will end up on someone else's menu!

A woodlousy life

Along with the millipedes and centipedes, at the bottom of your garden live hundreds – no *thousands* – of woodlice. There are 50 different species of woodlice in Britain and they're all shy and nervous so make sure you read this book *quietly*. The most common species are the imaginatively named common woodlouse and the pill bug – not to be swallowed for a headache.

Ugly bug fact file

Name of creature:	Woodlouse
Where found:	Worldwide in damp, dark places where there is rotting material, e.g. slimy brown leaves.
Distinguishing features:	About 15 mm long with seven pairs of jointed legs and two feelers. Segmented armour around its body allowing it to move easily.

LEGS → ← FEELERS ← HEAD ARMOUR PLATED BODY

A pill bug can roll itself into a ball (but please don't try bouncing one) – the common woodlouse can't do this. Some people think woodlice are boring. But, as always, they are wrong. Woodlice are *horribly* interesting.

Ten terribly interesting facts about woodlice

1 Not a lot of people know this, but a woodlouse is *not* a louse! In fact, country people call woodlice some extremely un-boring names.

2 Woodlice have extremely interesting relatives. Crabs, shrimps, prawns, lobsters and woodlice are all part of the crustacean family. Many people are extremely interested in eating their seaside relatives. Not many people are interested in eating woodlice you might think . . . but you'd be wrong.

3 This is not a horrible habit but a delicious delicacy. Salted and fried woodlice are an African speciality. They eat them like crisps!

4 Woodlice themselves have a horribly boring diet, though. They prefer bits of rotting plants and moulds. It's not everyone's cup of tea. But somebody's got to eat it, otherwise we'd be knee deep in the stuff. And woodlice do liven up their diet with the odd interesting dish . . . like other woodlice for instance. Or their own droppings and their skin after they've shed it.

5 Woodlice start off as eggs in their mum's tummy pouch. Four weeks later they hatch as tiny woodlice. Baby woodlice live with their parents, which is an interesting way for an ugly bug to start life because most insect eggs are abandoned by their mothers. It's terrible, but true!

6 And woodlice lives are full of drama and excitement. They put most TV soaps to shame. Yes. Woodlice never go to bed early with a mug of cocoa. They get to sleep all day and go out every night. And then they break into your home.

7 You're most likely to see woodlice in wet weather, because the biggest danger for a woodlouse is drying out. Interestingly, every year millions of baby woodlice come to a sad and sticky end by simply shrivelling up.

8 Some woodlice live in horribly interesting places. One variety lives inside yellow ants' nests and eats their droppings. Another type of woodlouse lives by the seaside under piles of slippery rotting seaweed.

9 Woodlice have some interesting if deadly enemies. The most dangerous of these is the dreaded woodlouse spider. Once grabbed in the spider's pincer-like grip, a woodlouse is doomed. The spider injects its poison and the woodlouse dies in . . . seven seconds. Quite an interesting way to go.

10 And there are some horribly interesting woodlice pests. Such as the tiny worms that sometimes live inside them . . . and kill them. Or the disgusting fly larvae that creep into a woodlouse's body and eat it from the inside out.

Dare you make friends with . . . a woodlouse?

Woodlice may not be the masterminds of the ugly bug world, but they've learnt a trick or two about how to survive. So why not put your woodlouse to the test? Make a note of what it does, then try to work out for yourself what makes a woodlouse tick.

1 First, find your woodlouse under a stone or a log, or in a damp corner.

2 Get a piece of wood (like a ruler) and try and get your woodlouse to climb onto it at different angles. Does your woodlouse:

a walk off in the other direction

b easily climb onto the wood

c struggle to get onto the wood?

3 Get a box with half the lid cut off. Find out which half the woodlouse likes best.

a light

b shade

4 Tip your woodlouse onto a table top and poke it gently with the point of a pencil. This is a pretty scary thing to do to a woodlouse (it'll be scary for you, too, if you do it on the dinner table – at dinnertime). Does your woodlouse:

a roll up in a ball

b run away

c clamp down on the ground

d pretend to be dead

e produce a disgusting substance to put you off eating it?

5 Don't forget to pop your woodlouse back unharmed where you found it.

Did you discover . . . that your woodlouse could easily climb out of danger . . . it sheltered in the shade, so as not to dry out in the sun . . . it had various sneaky survival tricks when it sensed it was in danger of attack?

With such a collection of tricks up its many trouser legs you'd think we'd be even more overrun by woodlice than we are. Well, we would be – if it wasn't for competition from a group of bugs so ugly that they make the woodlouse seem cuddly. Enter the Insect Invaders!

Insect invaders

Seen from any point of view insects are a horribly important group of ugly bugs. Insects are the most varied, the most ruthless, the hungriest and according to some people the most disgusting life-form on the planet. There may be over 30 million varieties of insect. That's TEN times more than all the other types of animal *put together*.

Not surprisingly, you can find insects virtually anywhere you look. That's if you really want to look! It's also not surprising that they have a big effect on our lives. And it's mainly as invaders – of crops, homes, schools. . . Nowhere is safe from the insect invaders!

Insect bits and pieces

Despite their many differences, insects have the same basic features. We have arranged for this cute little beetle to have a nasty little accident. . .

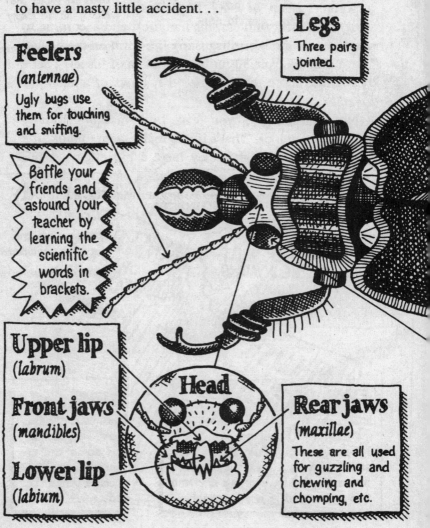

Legs
Three pairs jointed.

Feelers
(*antennae*)
Ugly bugs use them for touching and sniffing.

Baffle your friends and astound your teacher by learning the scientific words in brackets.

Upper lip
(*labrum*)

Front jaws
(*mandibles*)

Lower lip
(*labium*)

Head

Rear jaws
(*maxillae*)
These are all used for guzzling and chewing and chomping, etc.

Skin

Light, water-proof and tough. It doesn't stretch much and every so often the bug has to shed its skin to grow.

Breathing holes (spiracles)

Lead to tubes that carry air to every bit of the body.

Rear body (abdomen)

Contains guts and egg-laying equipment

Eyes

Insects see lots of little pictures – it's a bit like watching hundreds of TV screens except they are six sided and none gives a good picture. But they are good for spotting anything that moves and is worth eating!

Wings

Most insects have them. They go up and down and are controlled by the muscles inside the body.

Revolting insect records

1 Longest insect Giant stick insects from Borneo look like ugly old sticks. And they grow to a whopping 33 cm (13 inches) long.

YIKES!

2 Largest flying insect The Queen Alexandra's birdwing butterfly from New Guinea boasts a wing-span of 28 cm (11 inches). But that's nothing – a mere 300 million years ago there were giant dragonflies with wing-spans of 75 cm (30 inches)!

3 Smallest insects Cute little fairy flies are actually tiny wasps only 0.21mm long. The good news is, they don't sting humans.

4 Heaviest insect A single Goliath beetle from central Africa can weigh up to 100 grams.

5 Lightest insect The lightest insect is a species of parasitic wasp. It would take 25 million of them to weigh as much as one Goliath beetle!

6 Fastest flying insect There's a species of Australian dragonfly that can reach 58 km (36 miles) per hour.

58

7 Fastest breeding insects Aphid females give birth to live young. Inside these are developing bugs. Inside the developing bugs there are more developing bugs, and so on. Not surprisingly, in a single summer one female aphid can produce millions of descendants.

I'M ALREADY A GREAT GRANDMOTHER AND I WAS ONLY BORN THREE WEEKS AGO!

Horrible insect habits

Some ugly bugs only change a bit as they grow up and some change completely – so there are two types of horrible insect habits.

Horrible habits 1

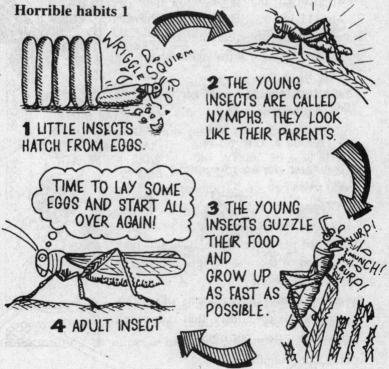

WRIGGLE SQUIRM

1 LITTLE INSECTS HATCH FROM EGGS.

2 THE YOUNG INSECTS ARE CALLED NYMPHS. THEY LOOK LIKE THEIR PARENTS.

TIME TO LAY SOME EGGS AND START ALL OVER AGAIN!

4 ADULT INSECT

3 THE YOUNG INSECTS GUZZLE THEIR FOOD AND GROW UP AS FAST AS POSSIBLE.

SLURP! MUNCH! BURP!

59

The scientific name for this collection of habits is "incomplete metamorphosis" (met-a-more-foe-sis). This describes a changing body. Mantids, locusts, dragonflies develop like this.

Horrible habits 2

1 LITTLE INSECTS HATCH FROM EGGS

2 THEY DON'T LOOK LIKE THEIR PARENTS. INSTEAD THEY ARE REVOLTINGLY WRIGGLING THINGS CALLED GRUBS OR LARVAE. THESE CREATURES MAY EAT COMPLETELY DIFFERENT FOOD FROM THEIR PARENTS AND LIVE IN PLACES THEIR PARENTS WOULDN'T BE SEEN DEAD IN.

3 THE YOUNG GRUBS GUZZLE THEIR FOOD AND GROW UP AS FAST AS POSSIBLE.

4 THEY GO INTO HIDING IN A LITTLE CASE OR COCOON AND THEY COME OUT AS ADULT UGLY BUGS.

The scientific name for this hideous habit is "complete metamorphosis". Beetles, ants, bees and wasps, butterflies and moths, flies and mosquitoes go through a complete metamorphosis.

Terrible table manners

Would you like to go to dinner with an insect? If so, you'd better learn how to eat like one.

What you need

a new sponge

tape

a drinking straw

a saucer of orange juice

What to do

1 Cut a small piece from the sponge.

2 Tape it to the end of the drinking straw.

3 Try to suck up a saucer of orange juice.

Congratulations! You're eating like a fly. Flies also sick up digestive juice. It helps them to dissolve their food before they slurp it up! (Don't try this!)

Too horrible to watch

Films are full of insects – especially scary films. There are giant ants and giant flies. And it's amazing how many space monsters look like insects.

In fact, film designers often study ugly bugs to get good ideas for a really ugly monster.

But who needs made-up insect monsters when some real-life insects are far more creepy?

First prize for creepiness Diopsid flies can see round corners because their eyes are on long stalks.

Second prize for creepiness There's a type of weevil that has a neck as long as the rest of its body. And no one knows why it's so long!

# Horrible beetles

Most people think that beetles look horribly ugly. Especially big black beetles that run over your foot and seem to enjoy it. The bad news is that of all the many orders of insects, beetles are the biggest group. And it's getting bigger because scientists are always discovering new species! Amazingly enough there is only one basic design for a beetle body.

Fearsome fact file

Name of creature:	Beetle
Where found:	Worldwide. Found just about anywhere you can imagine except in the sea, although some beetles live on beaches.
Distinguishing features:	Most beetles have short feelers. Folded fore-wings over the hind wings protect the beastly beetle body.

UGLY FACE → ← FOUL FEELERS

PROTECTIVE COVERING

CREEPY LEGS

Unbelievable beetles

With so many species of beetle it's inevitable that some of them are horribly amazing. And some of them have unbelievably horrible effects on human homes and food. But which of these beetles are too unbelievable to be true?

True or false?

1 The biscuit beetle eats, would you believe, biscuits. That's the bad news. The good news is that it doesn't like chocolate biscuits – only those nasty digestives you don't eat anyway. True/false

... AND THERE'S A PACKET OF 'RICH TEA' ON THE SHELF ABOVE WHEN WE'VE FINISHED THIS LOT

2 The cigarette beetle eats (howls of amazement) cigarettes. Its larvae especially like the tobacco and they never take any notice of the health warnings. True/false

3 The violin beetle *doesn't* eat violins – it just looks like a violin with legs. It lives amongst layers of fungus in trees in Indonesia. True/false

PLAY US A TUNE

OH! HA! HA! VERY FUNNY

4 The ice-cream beetle used to live in the Arctic where it ate small flies. More recently it has become a pest of cold stores where its favourite food is tutti-frutti ice-cream. True/false

5 "Tippling Tommy" is the nickname for a beetle that bores holes in wine and rum barrels. Tippling Tommy is actually a teetotaller. That's to say it never touches the alcohol inside the barrels – it prefers the wood! True/false

6 The drug store beetle is the name given to a biscuit beetle that lives in medicine cabinets. It enjoys slurping up some medicines, including many poisons! True/false

7 The giant gargling beetle is a rainforest beetle that takes a mouthful of dew and makes a loud gargling sound first thing in the morning. True/false

8 The bacon beetle beats you to breakfast every time by looting your larder in the night and munching your meats. Its favourite food is – you guessed it . . . bacon! True/false

9 The museum beetle is so fond of living in the past that it lives in dusty old display cases and eats museum specimens. Its favourite food . . . preserved ugly bugs. True/false

10 Deathwatch beetles live in wood. Some English churches contain families of beetles that have lived there for hundreds of years. True/false

Dare YOU make friends with . . . a ladybird?

One kind of beetle that definitely does exist is the ladybird. If you've ever wanted to get to know one socially this is your opportunity.

1 First look for some tempting aphids. They can be white, brown or black "greenfly" which you'll find on your rose bushes and other plants in summer.

2 Break off a small branch or leaves swarming with aphids and place the lot in a jam jar.

3 Add a ladybird. You can find them from the late spring onwards on bushes and fences. Watch your ladybird get to work. Lovely ladybirds can gobble up 100 greenfly a day.

4 Handle your ladybird gently and let it go after lunch. Do you really want to know what happens if things go wrong and your date gets upset? Try tickling it *very* gently with a leaf of grass. It will produce nasty tasting liquid. This will definitely put you off eating it. If you tickle it more it will roll on its back and pretend to be dead – a quick way to end your lunch date. If you upset it a lot it will bite. And beware, they *do* bite!

How not to upset a ladybird

During lunch you can discuss any subject with the ladybird without causing offence. This is because ladybirds don't understand English. Silly rhymes such as . . .

Ladybird, ladybird
Fly away home!
Your house is on fire
And your children are gone!

NOT THAT OLD CHESTNUT AGAIN!

. . . will not offend your ladybird in the least. This is also because:

1 Ladybirds don't have homes. A sheltered leaf is good enough for them. So it is unlikely they would be bothered if their home *was* on fire.

2 Ladybirds can fly but no ladybird would ever fly towards a fire. (Only maniac moths do that.)

3 Ladybirds don't give two hoots for their children. Once their eggs are laid, that's that!

Got a tough job? Get a beetle to do it

Beetles don't only come in a horrible variety of shapes and sizes. They also have a mind-boggling array of lifestyles, and where there's a job to be done there's a beetle at the ready.

BEWARE IT'S A BOMBARDIER!

Get yourself the ultimate in personal self-defence systems! Beat off the bullies with a bombardier beetle gun. Unique self-mixing action for nasty boiling chemicals. Amazing internal heating system in abdomen heats chemicals to temperature of 100°C and fires at 500 to 1000 squirts a second!

The bombardier beetle gun is maintenance free. Just let it crunch on a few smaller insects now and then.

ELM BARK BEETLE TREE SURGEON

Unsightly elm trees getting you down? Need a bit more light? Call us now. Try our unique Dutch elm disease fungus formula – a revolting little rootless plant that terminates trees. We'll soon get in under the bark and wipe out the woody weeds!
▷ Forest felled.
▷ No job too large.
Disease established in UK – 1970s. Over 25 million elms eliminated.

BRIGHTEN UP YOUR HOME

With a firefly lantern. As used in Brazil, the West Indies and Far East Firefly lanterns cast a soft green or yellow light from the bodies of female fireflies. Forty fireflies are as bright as one candle. They need no power or batteries – it's all done with chemicals by your friendly firefly.

THIS LOOKS LIKE A JOB FOR SUPERSEXTON!

Sexton Beetle
and Sons and Daughters

Dead? Just call in your friendly family funeral directors. No job too large. We'll bury anything even if it means ten hour shifts. Free personal limb chopping service to make burials easier. Professional after-care service. Our little grubs will look after the grave. No fee charged but they do like to come to the funeral feast. That's to feast on the dead body of course!

NEED ANY DUNG SHIFTED?

Scarab Beetle Services will get rid of the lot. Dung ball rolling and burying our speciality. What's more we'll even lay our eggs on it and get our grubs to eat it!

'Scarab beetles were round before the dung hit the ground They had 7,000 on the job and soon got rid of it all! My savannah has never looked tidier.' A.N.Elephant, Africa.

JEWELLERY WITH A MIND OF IT'S OWN

Ever wanted some jewellery that puts itself away at night? Buy some living jewel beetle jewellery as worn in many parts of the world. Choice of beautiful metallic colours including gold. Breaks the ice at parties, e.g. 'And what would your earring like to eat?' Manufacturer's warning: Don't allow your jewellery to lay eggs on your furniture. The grubs can lunch on your lounge suite for up to 47 years before turning into more jewel beetles.

Beetle battles

Beetles don't have much of a family life, but they take proper care of their property – if they don't, they'll soon find themselves in big trouble.

Stag Beetle Wrestling

If you were a male stag beetle, this is how you would defend your territory (your territory would be a bit of a tree branch). The aim of the game is to drop your opponent off the branch. . .

You will need:

a pair of giant jaws that look like deer antlers

What to do:

1 Eye up your opponent.

2 Grab him round the middle with your jagged jaws and try to flip him on to his back – that's easier said than done when he's trying to do the same to you. . .

3 If you lose, *you* fall off the branch and land on your back, where you risk being dissected and chewed by a waiting bunch of . . . awesome ants.

Awesome ants

Everyone knows about ants. They're easy enough to identify in the summer when they march into your home to inspect your kitchen. Ants can be pretty awful – they get everywhere from your plants to your pants – but they can be awesome, too, in all sorts of horrible ways.

Ugly bug fact file

Name of creature:	Ant
Where found:	Worldwide on land. They always live in nests.
Distinguishing features:	Most ants are less than 1 cm long. Narrow waist between thorax and abdomen. Angled feelers.

FEELERS   WAIST   ← RIDICULOUSLY FAT ABDOMEN

ANT

Awesome ant antics

1 Since 1880 German law has protected red ants' nests from destruction. Why? Because the ants from each nest eat an awesome 100,000 caterpillars and other ugly pests every day.

2 Honeypot ants squeeze sticky honeydew from aphids. They're doing the aphids a favour, *they* don't need the sickly stuff. The ants keep feeding this honeydew to particular ants in their nest to make them swell up like little beads. The swollen ants then sick up the honeydew to feed the rest of the nest. Awful!

SHE'S GOING TO BE SICK ~ DINNER TIME EVERYONE!

3 Weaver ants make their own tents from leaves sewn together with silk. Their larvae produce the silk and the awesome ants use their young as living shuttles – weaving them backwards and forwards! The adult ants just have to touch their larvae with their feelers whenever they need a bit more silk.

4 South American trap-jaw ants have huge long jaws. (Well, they're huge by ant standards.) They catch little jumping insects called springtails in their jaws and then inject them with poison.

But what's really awesome about these ants is that they also carry their eggs, or larvae, in those gruesome jaws as gently as any mother carries her baby – isn't that nice!

5 Leaf-cutter ants grow their own crops. The ants cut up the vegetation and mix it up with their droppings to make fertiliser. Then they grow fungus on it for food. They even weed unwanted kinds of fungus from their garden and put it on their compost heap. When a leaf-cutter

queen leaves to start a new nest she always takes a bit of
fungus with her to start a new garden.

HANG ON YOUR MAJESTY ~
HAVEN'T YOU FORGOTTEN
SOMETHING?

FESTERING
FUNGUS

6 And after the hard work of farming comes the harvest.
Harvester ants live in the desert where they gather seed
grains and make bread by chewing it all up and removing
the husks. The ants store their bread until they get hungry.

LET'S STORE IT BEFORE
IT TURNS TO TOAST!

7 The Australian bulldog ant has an awfully ugly bite.
Not only is the bite painful but this appalling ant then
squirts acid into the wound! Thirty bites can kill a human
in 15 minutes. This is probably the most dangerous ant in
the world. . .
8 Or is it? In the jungles of Africa and South America
lurks something even more awesome. It's 100 metres
(109 yards) long and 2 metres (7 feet) wide. It eats
anything foolish enough to get in its way. It reduces
lizards, snakes and even larger animals to skeletons. And

even big strong humans run for their lives rather than face it. Nothing can fight against it and live. What is this terrifying creature? Is it an ant? Well yes, actually, it's a column of 20 million army ants. The ants have no settled home. They spend their time invading places and being awesomely awful to any creature that gets in their way. If you live in South America it could get rid of cockroaches in your home, but you'd have to get yourself out of the way first.

9 Red South American Amazon ants fight fierce battles against their deadly enemies – the black ants. Red ant foot patrols are sent out to find a way into the enemy nest. They leave a trail for the main army to follow. The main army attacks and the Amazon ants use their curved jaws to slice off the heads of the opposing black ants. Some of the Amazon ants spray gases to further confuse the black ants. Then the Amazon ants retreat with their prisoners – the black ant grubs.

QUICK – EVERYONE GRAB A GRUB!

The grubs quickly pick up the smell of the Amazon ants and this fools them into thinking they're red ants too! But they aren't, and the poor befuddled black ants spend the rest of their lives as slaves to the awesome Amazon ants.

10. Marauder ants in Indonesia even build their own roads. These roads are often as long as 90 metres (98 yards) – and if you're ant-sized, that's *awesome*. Some of the roads even have soil roofs to protect them. And the ants have to follow a strict highway code:

A Always keep to your own part of the road. Returning ants in the middle, outwards ants at the edges.

B Move anything that gets in your way. If it's big, gnaw it. If it's small, get the younger ants to carry it off the road. If it's edible, bring it back to the nest (100 workers can shift one earthworm, 30 workers can shift one seed.)

WHAT'S HAPPENING?

C If you cross any other ant roads . . . kill the other ants. All ugly bugs that get in the way must be eaten alive.

CAN WE TALK ABOUT THIS?

Bet you never knew
There are 10,000 species of ant. But they do have some things in common.

- *An ant nest is ruled by a queen who spends her life laying eggs.*
- *All the ordinary "worker" ants are female.*
- *Males only hatch out at mating time and they die once they have mated!*

An Intellig-ant man

Almost as awesome as the ants themselves, are some of the humans who studied them. Take Baron Lubbock, for example. . .

But all this was nothing compared to his life-long love affair – with insects.

The barmy baron devised an awesome ant experiment. . .

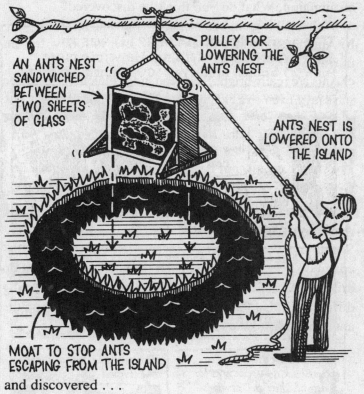

AN ANT'S NEST SANDWICHED BETWEEN TWO SHEETS OF GLASS

PULLEY FOR LOWERING THE ANTS NEST

ANTS NEST IS LOWERED ONTO THE ISLAND

MOAT TO STOP ANTS ESCAPING FROM THE ISLAND

and discovered . . .

1 Ants can be ancient. Worker ants can live for seven years, and queen ants for 14 years before they die of old age.

2 Ants respond strangely to sounds – they listen through their legs!

3 Tiny ugly bugs hide in ants nests.

He devised another ant experiment . . . with mazes, obstacle courses and a table with movable rings – all ant-sized, of course. He wanted to find out if ants had a sense of direction. What do you think he discovered?

a) We're talking ant brains here – the ants all got lost.

b) Ants are a bit like sheep – they always follow the ant in front.

c) Ants are really bright. They can judge directions using the sun's rays, even on a cloudy day – so they found their way out.

Answers: a) False. **b)** Partly true. Ants do follow one another – the leading ant makes a trail for the others to follow. **c)** Amazing but true. Ants are better at finding their way than some humans.

Ant Aromas

Scents are very important to ants. Scientists have discovered several ant scents each of which makes ants do different things. Imagine you were a scientist observing different kinds of ant behaviour. Could you match up the ant behaviour to the smell that causes it?

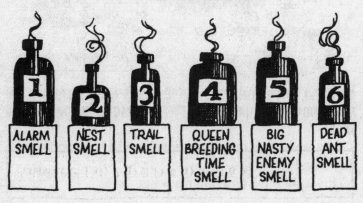

a) THE ANTS TRY TO BURY YOU IN AN ANT CEMETERY

b) THE ANTS RUN AWAY FROM THEIR NEST

c) AN ANT ARMY IS SUMMONED

d) SOME ANTS TRY TO RUN AND OTHERS STAY TO FIGHT

e) ANTS FIGHT EACH OTHER

f) THE ANTS FIND THEIR WAY HOME

g) THE ANTS DON'T DO ANYTHING IF YOU HAVE THIS SMELL

h) MALE ANTS ARE ATTRACTED BY THIS SMELL

Answers: 1 d) 2 g) 3 f) 4 h) 5 b) 6 a)

79

Sleazy bees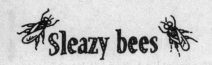

Ants and bees belong to the same gruesome group of ugly bugs. So it's no surprise to find some bee species live in nests ruled by queens. Humans tend to say that bees are "good" because they make honey – but bees can be bad in their own horrible way. You'll get a buzz (ha ha) out of teaching your teacher their ugly secrets.

Ugly bug fact file

Name of creature:	Bees and wasps
Where found:	Worldwide. Most bees live on their own. Only a few species live in large nests.
Horrible habits:	They sting people.
Any helpful habits:	Bees make honey and pollinate flowers.
Distinguishing features:	Thin waist between thorax and abdomen. Four transparent wings. Bees have long tongues and often carry yellow lumps of pollen on their hind legs.

WAIST

NASTY STINGY BIT

POLLEN

BEE

TONGUE

Inside the beehive

Bees that live together in nests are called "social bees". Well, you'd have to be social to live with *this* lot.

Quarrelling queens Usually there's just one queen in a hive. She spends her time laying eggs. But sometimes more than one queen hatches out, and things can turn rather nasty. The first queen to appear kills off any rivals.

Drowsy drones It's a lovely life for a drone. Your worker sisters keep house for you. And they even feed you. You don't have a sting because you never need to fight anyone. There's just one problem. You've got to battle with hundreds of brothers for a chance to mate. If you mate with a queen you die.

Weary workers What do the workers do? Well, (funnily enough) they work. And they work. And they work. In a few short weeks the worn-out workers work themselves to death!

ME NEXT! MOVE OVER!

DON'T PUSH IN!

JOBS FOR WORKERS

clean the hive • nurse the grubs • guard the nest • fetch pollen and nectar from flowers • make honey • feed the queen • feed the grubs • feed the drones • make wax (it oozes from the worker's bodies) • build new cells using wax

Horrible honey

So you love honey. Doesn't the thought of a lovely honey sandwich make your mouth water? And NOTHING is going to put you off it – right? RIGHT. Here's how bees make honey – complete with the horrible details.

1 Bees make honey from the sweet nectar produced by flowers. It's horribly hard work. Some bees collect from 10,000 flowers a day. They often visit up to 64 million flowers to make just 1 kg of honey.

2 That's good news for the flowers because the busy bees also pick up pollen. They even have little leg baskets to carry it. The bee takes the pollen to another flower of the same type. There, some of the precious pollen brushes on to the flower, fertilises it and so helps it form a seed.

POLLEN BASKETS

3 Why do you think the flower goes to all the bother of making scents, bright colours and nectar. Is it all for us? No! It's to attract bees. Lots of bees means lots of flowers. See?

4 A bee uses her long tongue and a pump in her head to suck up nectar. She stores the nectar in a special stomach.

LONG SLIMY TONGUE

5 Nectar is mostly water. To get rid of the water, bees sick up the nectar and dry it out on their tongues – ugh.

6 Then they store the honey in honeycomb cells until they need it. That's unless humans steal it for their sandwiches!

Beewilder some bees

It's best done on a summer's day in a garden terrace or park where there are lots of bees.

1 Put out a vase of flowers. Watch the bees find the flowers and go off to tell their friends.

BUZZ

BUZZ

2 Meanwhile you hide the flowers.

3 Back come some more bees. They are humming with happiness at the thought of all that lovely nectar and pollen.

HAPPY BUZZ

4 But there are no flowers. Result: Bewildered bees.

???

Bees bee-ware

Bees have lots of horrible enemies. To stop them, every hive has its guards. The guards don't receive training but if they did it might look like this . . .

 Honey-bee As long as they've got some food you let them in. If not, chase them away! Bee careful. Bees from other hives sometimes steal our honey!

Death's-head hawk moth This nastily-named night raider flies into our hive. It licks our lovely honey with its terribly long tongue. Bee on your guard after dark!

 African honey-badger This hairy horror breaks open our honeycomb with its long claws. It makes shocking stinks to drive away our guards. STING ON SIGHT!

Blister-beetle grub Bee careful when you visit flowers. This greedy grub will ambush you! It hitches a free ride to our hive. Then it hides in our cells and guzzles our grubs.

 Mouse Another horrible honey hunter. STING TO DEATH! Getting rid of the mouse's body is a bit of a bother. It's too big to move. Cover the body with gooey gum from trees. The gum will mummify the mouse and stop it stinking!

Humans They only want us for our honey and our bees' wax for polish and candles. Sting them if they get too close. You can't pull your sting from their skin. If you try it'll drag your insides out. Never mind – you'll die a hero!

 Cuckoo bee Don't be a cuckoo and let them in. It's easy to think they're one of us. But once inside they'll lay their ugly eggs.

Pretty Uglies

What better on a summer's day than to laze about with a cool drink and watch the butterflies flutter past! And isn't it amazing that there are thousands of different kinds of butterfly throughout the world in an incredible variety of shapes and forms. Pity about their horrible habits and the even more gruesome things they got up to when they were caterpillars!

Ugly bug fact file

PROBOSCIS →

BUTTERFLY

Name of creature:	Butterfly
Where found:	Worldwide. The larger butterflies live in tropical countries.
Horrible habits:	Caterpillars eat our vegetables.
Any helpful habits:	Butterflies pollinate flowers and look pretty.
Distinguishing features:	Two pairs of wings, often highly colourful. Narrow body. Long, coiled feeding tube (proboscis) attached to mouth.

85

The good, the bad and the ugly

The good

1 Butterflies and many moths have amazing coloured patterns on their wings. These colours are made up of tiny overlapping scales and they help male and female butterflies to find each other before mating.

2 Butterflies and moths can detect smells using their antennae. The male Indian moon moth can scent a female over 5 km (3 miles) away. It follows the scent through woods – round trees and across streams – ignoring all other smells. That's like you sniffing your supper 75 km (47 miles) away!

3 Butterflies can smell through their feet! That way they can land on a leaf and know what type it is. Which helps female butterflies to lay their eggs on leaves their caterpillars can happily eat.

The bad

1 Newly hatched *polyphemous* (polly-fee-mouse) moth caterpillars are tiny. But they start eating straight away and within 48 hours they increase their weight 80,000 times.

1 HOUR   24 HOURS   48 HOURS

That's bad news for the local greenery because the chomping caterpillars can strip all the leaves from a tree.

2 Common large white butterflies really are as common as muck. They fly across the English channel in swarms so vast that a big band of these bad butterflies once stopped a cricket match.

3 But if you're into vast swarms, the African migrant butterfly takes some beating. A scientist once tried to watch a crowd of them fly past. This was a bad idea because the procession continued for three months without stopping!

DAY 6: CAN'T GO ON MUCH LONGER...

And the ugly

1 Ugly scenes have been reported when butterflies get drunk. It's true – the juices from rotting fruit are slightly alcoholic and even one slurp's too much for a butterfly. It flops and droops around on the ground.

2 The gruesome death's-head hawk moth (last seen stealing into beehives) has a sinister skull shape on its thorax. Its equally ugly caterpillars like to nibble the poisonous deadly-nightshade plant. The noxious nightshade makes the caterpillars taste so terrible that no one in their right mind would ever want to eat them.

3 Brown-tail moth caterpillars are also pretty ugly. Their bodies are covered in sharp needle-like hairs that break off in your skin and make it itch like mad.

Could *you* be a large blue butterfly?

The large blue butterfly is – amazingly enough, a large, blue butterfly. In Britain it is very rare and is currently only found in a few places in the west country. Large blue butterflies are also found in France and Central Europe.

Like all butterflies, the large blue begins life as an egg that hatches into a caterpillar that turns into a chrysalis that turns into a butterfly. But it does horribly odd things on the way. Imagine you were a large blue butterfly. Would you survive?

1 You hatch out. How do you get rid of the remains of your egg?
a) Eat it.
b) Bury it.
c) Throw it at a passing wasp.
2 You live on a wild thyme or marjoram plant. Suddenly your plant is invaded by another large blue caterpillar that starts eating your leaves. What do you do?
a) Agree to share the plant.
b) Eat the rival caterpillar.
c) Hide until it's gone away.
3 After guzzling all the leaves you can, and shedding your skin three times, you fall off your plant. As you amble along, an ant suddenly appears. What do you do?
a) Persuade it to give you a cuddle – then give it some honey in return.
b) Grip its feelers and refuse to let go.
c) Roll over and pretend to be dead.
4 The ant takes you to its nest. It shoves you in a chamber with the ant grubs. What do you do next?

a) Make friends with them.

b) Raid the ants' food supplies and help yourself.

c) Eat the ant grubs.

5 You spend the winter sleeping in the ants' nest. Soon after you wake you hang yourself from the ceiling and turn into a chrysalis. About three weeks later you fall on the floor and crawl out of your nasty damp chrysalis. Congratulations – you're now an adult butterfly! But how do you escape from the ants' nest?

a) You have to dig an escape tunnel.

b) You crawl your way out all by yourself.

c) You pretend to be dead and an ant carries you out.

6 Free at last! What's the first thing you do?

a) Find something to eat – a dead ant will do.

b) Find a mate.

c) Dry out your brand new wet wings.

And then you fly off to enjoy your new life! Make the best of it – you've only got 15 days to live!

MUM, WHY IS THIS ANT LICKING ME?

IT'S A LONG STORY!

89

Barmy beliefs and strange scientists

For hundreds of years no one knew exactly where caterpillars came from. And there were some pretty strange suggestions. Here's the Roman writer Pliny...

DEW FALLS FROM TREES IN SPRING AND TURNS INTO CATERPILLARS.

But no one realised that caterpillars were anything to do with butterflies. Then in the seventeenth century, the microscope was invented. All over Europe scientists started to observe insects in gruesome close-up detail.

One of these scientists was Jan Swammerdam (1637-1680) who lived in Holland. As a young man he studied medicine. But he much preferred studying insects to humans! His work was very delicate and he even used tiny scissors that had to be sharpened under a microscope. One day he cut open a cocoon and found... mixed up gooey bits of butterfly. Jan had proved that caterpillars turn into butterflies.

But people didn't believe him. The introduction to his insects book, written in 1669, didn't help either. Swammerdam said that the way insects changed their form was...

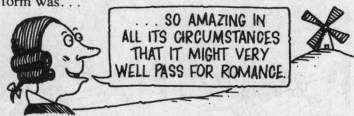

... SO AMAZING IN ALL ITS CIRCUMSTANCES THAT IT MIGHT VERY WELL PASS FOR ROMANCE.

But as more scientists studied butterflies they discovered that Jan was quite right. These scientists were the first lepidopterists – a horribly complicated name for people who study butterflies and moths.

Lethal lepidopterists

Nowadays lepidopterists are mild-mannered folk who enjoy observing and photographing butterflies in what is left of their natural surroundings. It wasn't always like that.

1 In the eighteenth century, fashionable ladies wore brightly coloured butterfly and moth wings as *jewellery*.

2 Traditional butterfly hunters raced after butterflies with big nets shouting, "There she goes!" When they caught an unfortunate flutterer they plunged it into a bottle of poison and pinned it to a board – *horrible!*

3 In the nineteenth century, hunters collected hundreds of butterflies from tropical forests in New Guinea. When the butterflies soared too high they fired guns loaded with fine shot to bring them down!

4 The British collector, James Joicey, spent a fortune over 30 years paying people to collect butterflies for him. By 1927 this millionaire's son had run out of cash. But when Joicey died in 1932 his collection numbered 1,500,000 dead butterflies.

Is your teacher a lepidopterist?
Find out the easy way with this teacher-teasing test.

1 How can you always tell a moth from a butterfly?
a) Moths come out at night and butterflies in the day.
b) Moths rest with their wings flat. Butterflies rest with their wings upright.
c) Moths don't have knobs on their antennae.

2 How does a hairstreak butterfly avoid having its head bitten off?
a) It has a dummy head.
b) It has a head with armour on it.
c) It bites first.

3 Silk comes from the cocoons spun by the silkworm moth caterpillar. According to legend this was discovered by a Chinese Empress in 2640 BC. But how did she make her discovery?

a)  **b)** **c)**

a) By careful scientific observation.
b) Her cat brought in a cocoon to show her.
c) A cocoon fell into her cup of tea.

4 Where does a cigar-case bearer caterpillar live?
a) In a cigar case.
b) In a little house made of bits of plants joined with silk.
c) In the fur of animals.
5 How can you tell when a butterfly is old?
a) Ragged wings
b) It goes grey.
c) Droopy feelers

I LOOK MORE LIKE A CABBAGE GREY!

Savage spiders

The horrible thing about spiders is that you can't get away from them. You can see their webs on plants and washing lines and in garden sheds. And when you come home you'll probably find spiders hiding there too. Spiders aren't insects but that doesn't make them any less horrible. In fact, more people are scared of spiders than are scared of insects. Maybe it's because spiders have some seriously savage habits.

Ugly bug fact file

Name of creature:	Spider
Where found:	Worldwide. On land and in fresh water.
Horrible habits:	Paralyses prey with poison fangs and sucks out the juices.
Any helpful habits:	Keeps down the numbers of insects.
Distinguishing features:	Head and thorax joined. Separate abdomen. Four pairs of jointed legs. Eight eyes. Produces silk. Inside is a breathing organ called a book lung

SEPARATE ABDOMEN

EIGHT HORRIBLE HAIRY LEGS

EYES

HEAD AND CHEST JOINED

Spiders can't always be savage, surely? They care for their young – sometimes. Mummy wolf-spiders often carry baby spiders on their backs. Ah, how sweet. It's a pity mum eats dad and the babies eat each other. And then there are the *really* savage bits. Read on at your own risk!

Teacher's terror test

Turn the tables on your teacher as you test his terror tolerance.

EIGHT WALKING STICKS – HE MUST BE OLD!

1 How do spiders avoid getting caught in their own webs?

a) nifty footwork

b) They have oily non-stick feet.

c) They slide down a line and pulley.

2 How long can a spider live?

a) six months

b) 25 years

c) 75 years

3 When a spider sheds its skin what parts does it get rid of?

a) its skin

b) the front of its eyes

c) The lining of its guts and book lung (breathing organ).

4 What does a spider do with its old web?

a) wear it

b) throw it away

c) eat it

5 What does a spitting spider do?

a) It spits a poison that kills its victims as they try to escape.

b) It lassoes its victims with a 10 cm squirt of silk that ties them to the ground.

c) Nothing. It sits around looking strangely sinister.

6 How do small spiders fly through the air?

a) They use electricity in the atmosphere.

b) They inflate their bodies like tiny balloons.

c) They spin little silk parachutes.

7 What, according to legend, is the best way to cure the bite of a tarantula spider?

a) a cup of tea

b) a lively folk dance

c) suck out the venom

8 How many spiders are there in one square metre (11 square feet) of grassland?

a) 27

b) 500

c) 1,795

9 How does a spider get into your bath?

a) It crawls up the drain-pipe but can't climb out of the bath.

b) It drops down from the ceiling but can't climb out of the bath.

c) It crawls out of the taps but can't climb out of the bath.

Answers: 1 b) 2 b) Tarantulas can live this long. **3** All of these! **4 c) 5 b) 6 c)** Sometimes its a length of silk and sometimes a silken loop that acts just like a parachute. **7 b)** A spider's bite is supposed to make you dance madly – that's called tarantism. The tarantella folk dance is supposed to cure a bite. **8 b)** Scientists reckon there are two billion spiders in England and Wales! **9 b)** The spider drops in for a drink of water. But the walls of the bath are too slippery for the spider to climb out again.

Savage spider file

So your teacher's terrified of spiders? Here are a few rational reasons why they're quite right to be scared.

The bird-eating spider - a terrifying tarantula

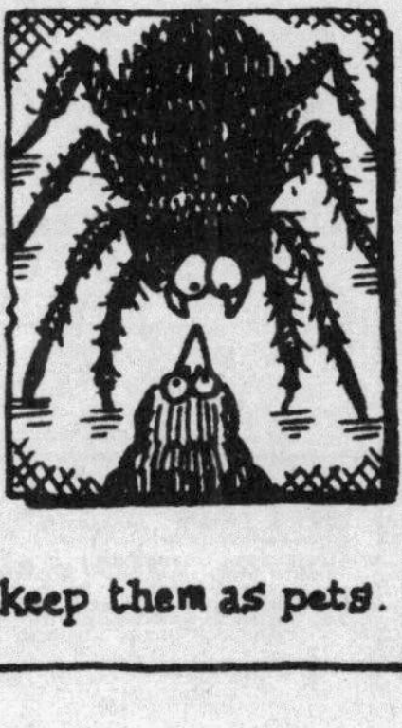

Description: Big. Can grow to 25cm (10inches) long including legs.

Lives in: South America

Fearsome features: Scarifyingly hairy

Marital status: Single

Horrible habits: Eats birds and frogs.

The bad news: It has a painful bite.

The Very bad news: Those hairs can give you a nasty rash.

The absolutely appalling news: People keep them as pets.

The black widow spider

Description: Body 2.5 cm (1 inch) long. Always in black with a sinister red mark on her underside.

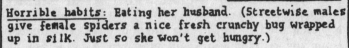

Lives in: Southern USA

Fearsome features: The most poisonous spider.

Marital status: Probably a widow

Horrible habits: Eating her husband. (Streetwise males give female spiders a nice fresh crunchy bug wrapped up in silk. Just so she won't get hungry.)

Redeeming features: Rarely bites people. A shy spider who doesn't like fighting and only bites if you come across her unexpectedly.

The bad news: She hides in places where you come across her unexpectedly.

The very bad news: Such as toilet seats.

The absolutely appalling news: And her poison is absolutely deadly. It's said to be 15 times deadlier than a rattlesnake's.

The wandering spider

Description: 12cm (5 inches) leg-span with hairy legs.

Lives in: Brazil

Fearsome features: Said to be the most dangerous spider in the world.

Marital status: No one dare ask.

Horrible habits: Comes into houses uninvited. Wanders around biting people.

Strange spider beliefs and even stranger scientists

Some spider scientists had strange ideas and others were involved in strange experiments. Spider science (arachnology) started with the Greeks. But Greek writer, Philostratus, had some rather strange ideas about spiders. He reckoned that spiders spun silk to keep warm. Nice try, Phil. Mind you, the Romans weren't much better. According to Pliny, spiders appeared from seeds that grew in rotting material.

Mad Mouffet We've all heard the rhyme about little Miss Muffet who got scared away by a great big spider. But did you know that she was a real person? Her name was Patience Mouffet and she was unfortunate enough to be the daughter of strange sixteenth-century spider scientist, Dr Thomas Mouffet. Why unfortunate? Well, her dad used to dose her with live spiders whenever she had a cold. As a special treat Patience got to eat mashed up spiders on toast.

Brave Baerg Dr WJ Baerg of Arkansas, USA conducted some strange experiments with the aim of discovering exactly how deadly a venomous spider bite really was. In 1922 he deliberately allowed himself to be bitten by a poisonous black widow spider! The first test was a failure – the spider wouldn't bite. So Dr B tried again and this time he was delighted to get a nasty nip. When he got out of hospital three days later the spider scientist recorded that he'd felt unbearable pain. Now, there's a surprise.

In 1958 Dr Baerg was at it again. This time he decided to test spider bites on guinea-pigs and rats rather than himself. But the intrepid investigator didn't escape pain altogether. He had an unhappy accident with a Trinidadean tarantula. Baerg was lining up the hairy horror to bite an unfortunate white rat when it bit him on the finger. (That's the spider not the rat.) Luckily Dr B found that the poison didn't harm him. So he allowed himself to get bitten by a Panamanian tarantula instead and this time suffered a stiff finger. So brave Dr Baerg concluded that tarantula bites weren't so bad after all!

Could YOU be a spider scientist?

Can you predict the result of this strange spider experiment?

In 1948 Professor Hans Peters noticed that garden spiders always spun their webs at 4 o'clock in the morning. So he fed some spiders with caffeine (that's the chemical in coffee that wakes people up) and others with sleeping pills to see what would happen. What do you think he discovered?

a) Spiders are affected just like us. The spiders stimulated with coffee woke up at 1.30am and then worked all night. The spiders drugged with sleeping pills slept until 10.35am.

b) Spiders are completely different from humans. The caffeine-stimulated spiders went to sleep. And the spiders drugged with sleeping pills worked harder than ever.

c) The urge to spin webs was stronger than any drug. The spiders made some odd-looking webs. But they continued to start work at 4am.

EXCELLENT – ANOTHER COFFEE BREAK!

Answer: c)

Bet you never knew!
Spiders have spun webs in space. On 28 July 1973 garden spiders Arabella and Anita boldly blasted off into space to visit the Skylab space station. Their mission – an experiment to find whether they could spin webs in zero gravity. Their first efforts were untidy. They weren't used to floating around weightless. Later efforts were more successful although poor Anita died in orbit.

Weird webs

Spiders spin silk to produce their intricate webs. The webs they make catch flies and other unlucky creatures. But the more you find out about webs the weirder they seem.

1 To make one web, spiders need to spin different types of silk.

- Dry silk a thousandth of a millimetre thick for the spokes of a web.
- Stretchy silk covered in gluey droplets for the rest. The sticky bits take in moisture and stop the web drying out.
- Other kinds of silk for wrapping up eggs and dead insects.

2 Webs come in many shapes and sizes. Have you ever seen any of these?

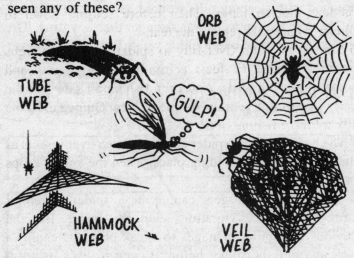

ORB WEB

TUBE WEB

GULP!

HAMMOCK WEB

VEIL WEB

3 The house spider makes a hammock-shaped web. The spider spits out bits of insect and leaves them lying around for someone else to tidy up – a horrible habit!

4 The trap-door spider digs a tunnel with a trap door at one end. The spider waits within. It grabs a passing insect

and pulls it down. The door closes and the innocent victim is never seen again.

SHUT THE DOOR LOVE – THERE'S A TERRIBLE DRAUGHT COMING DOWN THE TUNNEL!

5 The purse-web spider makes a purse-shaped web. This savage spider then stabs its victims through the web with its long poison fangs. Then before settling down to dinner it carefully repairs the tear.

6 Sinister *nephilia* (Nef-filly-a) spiders spin giant webs up to 2 metres (7 feet) across to catch insects and sometimes even birds. And even fish aren't safe – in the early part of this century people in New Guinea used the silk to make fishing nets!

7 The web-throwing spider chucks its web over insects as they work under its hiding place. Then the spider drops in for tea.

8 When an insect gets caught in a spider's web, it struggles and the vibrations alert the spider. But the devious ero spider manages to sneak on to its enemy's web and bite the spider before it even realises its got a visitor. Evil ero then sucks its victim dry and scurries away, leaving an empty spider husk sitting in its web!

9 In some places in California, spiders' webs fall like snow. The flakes are made up of mixed-up spiders' webs blown together by the wind.

103

Now you know *all* about them.

Dare YOU make friends with ... a spider?

To save spinning you own silk, try asking a spider to make some for you.

1 Cut a plastic lemonade bottle in half.

2 Add soil and twigs to the bottom half.

3 Now find your spider. Sheds and out-houses are good places to look. If you find a web the spider is normally hiding nearby. One spider is enough. Add two and one will eat the other! Be gentle, though – spiders are easily hurt!

4 Tape up the two halves of the bottle.

5 Feed your new friend with a small fly through the top of the bottle.

6 Check to see if she's spun any silk or made a web. If she has, go ahead and try knitting yourself a nice pair of spider silk gloves.

Biting bugs

For us humans the most horrible thing about insects is the way they bite us. And suck blood and sometimes give us horrible diseases too. Maybe that's why people call a crowd of insects a "plague". Plagues are deadly diseases. In the past 10,000 years more people have died from diseases carried by insects than any other single cause. *Help!*

Rogues' gallery

Here are the chief culprits.

Malarial mosquito

<u>Sex</u>: Female

<u>Habits</u>: Sucks blood before laying her eggs, while Mr Mosquito prefers plant juices.

<u>Weapons</u>: A long snout for sticking into people and a pump-action saliva gun to stop your blood setting.

<u>Last seen</u>: Sightings have been reported all over the world. Often loiters near water.

<u>Known crimes</u>: In hot countries her bite passes on germs that cause malaria. Victims suffer raging fever and feel very hot and then very cold. Responsible for one million deaths each year. Sometimes gives us yellow fever into the bargain.

<u>Danger rating</u>: Beware! Two billion people live in areas threatened by this brutal blood-sucker.

Body louse

Description: 1.5-3.5mm long. Has no wings.

Weapon: Blood-sucking tube

Habits: Sucks blood

Last seen: Hiding in the seams of clothes.

Known crimes: Disgusting droppings can contain germs that cause the deadly disease, typhus. The louse scratches human skin with its feet to let in the germs.

Danger rating: Nasty. But nothing that a good bath and clean clothes can't cure.

Known associates: Head lice, or "nits", live in hair. They quite like clean hair and happily hop from head to Head. (Yes. Head teachers can get them too!)

Tsetse fly

Habits: Sucks blood. Known to drink up to three times its own weight in a single sitting. Likes a challenge - enjoys biting through rhinoceros skin.

Last seen: Many parts of Africa.

Known crimes: Its bite passes on germs that cause sleeping sickness. This deadly disease causes fever, tiredness and death.

Danger rating: In Africa 50 million people are at risk plus countless cattle, camels, mules, horses, donkeys, pigs, goats, sheep, etc. etc. etc.

Benchuca (ben-chooka) bug

Last seen: South America

Habits: Creeps up on you at night and stabs you with its pointed snout. Sucks a bit of blood and scarpers before you squash it.

Known crimes: Spreads Chagas' disease. Result – tired and feverish humans.

It took humans many years of painstaking research to track down the culprits of these terrible diseases and to decide what to do about them.

Malaria mystery solved

In the nineteenth century Scottish born scientist Patrick Manson discovered how mosquitoes pass on malaria. Here's how he did it.

1 1894 Manson met Ronald Ross of the Indian Medical Service.

Hello Pat!

I think malaria is caused by tiny parasites. They live in mosquitoes.

2 So Ross went off to India to look for them.

3 1897. Ross found the parasites inside a mosquito.

Eureka!

4 1900. Manson wanted more proof. He sent two assistants off to spend three months living in a swamp full of mosquitoes.

Is this really such a good idea?

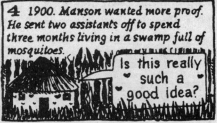

Plague puzzle

Some diseases were even more puzzling than malaria. Can you piece together the gruesome clues to unravel the cause of the deadly bubonic plague?

1346 It came from the East and in the next six years 25 million people died. Peasants died in their fields and in England three Archbishops of Canterbury died in a single year. People lived in terror of THE BLACK DEATH.

1855 The plague ravaged China. In 1894 it hit the Chinese ports and in Hong Kong the death toll soared. The harbour was crammed with steam ships. And these ships took the disease to Japan, Australia, South Africa and the Americas. The plague reached India and killed six million people in ten years.

1898 In Bombay, Dr Paul-Louis Simond of the Institut Pasteur was a worried man. The fearless French doctor had been sent to India to find the cause of the plague. Day and night he wrestled with the same fiendish puzzle. In the stricken city thousands of people were dying. All developed fist-sized bulges under their armpits followed by fever and death. But how and why?

Day after day Simond scoured the squalid streets in search of an answer. Everywhere he noticed dead rats – 75 in one house. It was extremely unusual to find so many dead rats all together in one place.

They must have died quite quickly but what had killed them? And why was it that any humans who touched the rats seemed to fall sick with the plague? These plague rats seemed to have more fleas than healthy rats. And the fleas bit people, too.

The monsoon rain buffeted the outside of the makeshift lab in a tent. Inside Simond risked his own health as he cut up the dead rats. Then he made a dramatic discovery. In the rat's blood he found the germs known to cause the plague.

But what was the cruel connection between rats, fleas and humans? At long last the answer came. The intrepid scientist had solved the most terrifying mystery of all time. That evening he wrote in his diary in a frenzy of excitement.

But what was that crucial connection?
a) A flea bites a rat and passes on the plague. The rat bites a human and passes on the plague.
b) A flea gets plague from biting an infected rat. The flea bites a human and passes on the plague.
c) A human gets plague from an infected flea bite. The plague-crazed human bites a rat and passed on the plague.

Answer:
b) Microbes multiply in the flea's gut until it can't feed. The hungry flea bites a human and injects millions of germs.

Although Simond had the answer it took another 20 years before scientists accepted that he was right. It wasn't until 1914 that they fully understood the effects of the plague on fleas. Already vaccines were being developed against the plague and these together with insecticides and rat poisons have reduced the danger of plague epidemics in the future.

Beat the bugs

Hopefully you can avoid getting a horrible disease from a biting bug. But it's hard to avoid getting bitten. Here are some danger zones.

1 Bed During the day bed bugs hide in cracks and behind wallpaper. Then at night out they pop for a midnight feast of blood.

2 Riverbanks Blackflies launch dawn and dusk raids.

3 Fields at dawn Ticks can lurk in the long grass. They prefer dogs for dinner but if one isn't handy they'll make do with you.

4 Bogs and marshes Millions of midges fly around seeking blood for breakfast. Close up they're too small to see clearly. You can't see their wings because in some varieties they beat at an awesome 62,760 strokes a minute. That's why some people call midges, "no-see-ums". But you know-um when they bite you.

Some remedies you wouldn't want to try.

1 Tsetse fly trap no. 1

Remedy: Keep a pet ox.

Notes: Scientists have found that the terrible tsetse is attracted to smelly ox breath. In Zimbabwe similar smelling chemicals lured thousands of tsetses into poisoned cloth traps.

Drawbacks: Smelly ox breath. Feeding your ox. Having to take it to school with you.

2 Tsetse fly trap no. 2

Remedy: Ferment some cassava.

Notes: In Zaire people make beer from cassava roots. The messy mixture produces carbon dioxide gas that lures the flies to their doom.

Drawbacks: People might start drinking your beer. This could cause embarrassing situations – especially at school.

3 Bed bug beaters

Remedy: Let loose an army of Pharaoh ants in your bedroom.

Notes: Pharoah ants eat bed bugs.

Drawbacks: How to get rid of the Pharaoh ants. Try smearing your duvet with jam. Or borrow an ant-eater.

GUZZLE
MUNCH!
GNASH
GOBBLE!
CHOMP!

4 Biting bug barbecue

Remedy: Light a really smoky bonfire.

BUT IT GOT RID OF THE BUGS SIR

Notes: Most biting bugs don't like smoke.

Drawbacks: Not a very sensible thing to do. Ever. Especially not recommended inside the home or at school.

5 Flea fighters

Remedy: Use flea mites to fight fleas.

OW! BIFF! OOF!

Notes: Tiny mites infest fleas in the same way that fleas infest people. All you need to do is to capture a flea and add some mites. (You need a microscope and a steady hand to do this.)

Drawbacks: Doesn't get rid of fleas. But it does give them a taste of their own medicine.

6 Pest poisoner

Remedy: Squirt biting bugs with DDT.

DDT

Notes: In the 1940s this insecticide was used to rid the southern USA and parts of Africa and South America of malarial mosquitoes.

Drawbacks: By 1950 two types of mosquito were immune to the powerful poison. Worse still, DDT harmed bug-eating animals and the animals that ate those animals. Note-humans still spend millions of pounds each year inventing new kinds of insecticide.

A remedy you might like to try

Some aromatic plant oils ward off insects. You can buy these oils from herbalists or natural cosmetics shops. You could try using citronella oil on a warm summer's evening...

1 Drip a few drops of the oil on a damp piece of cotton wool.

2 Put the cotton wool in a warm place indoors.

3 When the room is full of scent open the window and dare any biting bugs to come in!

Bet you never knew!

Ugly bugs invented insecticide. Traditional moth-balls are made from a herb called camphor. Long before humans discovered camphor, assassin bugs were feeding on the camphor weed and blowing camphor bubbles. They lay their eggs in the bubbles and the harmful herbal smell keeps other bugs at bay!

Devious disguises

As if escaping from spiders, fish, lizards, frogs, toads, small mammals and even horrible humans wasn't enough, insects seem to spend most of their time playing hide and seek with each other. And they don't just do it for fun. Insects have to eat, after all, and they don't want to get eaten. So they use some cruel and cunning tricks to get one up on their ugly bug enemies.

Bet you never knew!
Horrible hunter, the praying mantis really does look as though it's praying. It holds its forelegs together as it waits for a tasty snack to pass by. Its forelegs have a jagged edge, just like a saw blade. The praying mantis will catch and skewer its bug lunch in just a twentieth of a second – then bite off its ugly little head!

Insect survival

If you were an insect, would you stay alive? Try this crash course in survival skills to help you decide.
Tactic Number 1: Pretend to be Something Else
You've obviously got an advantage if you already look like something else – and quite a few insects do. Which of these ordinary objects might really be insects?
a) a leaf
b) a sweet wrapper
c) a twig
d) a stick

115

e) a thorn
f) a bird dropping

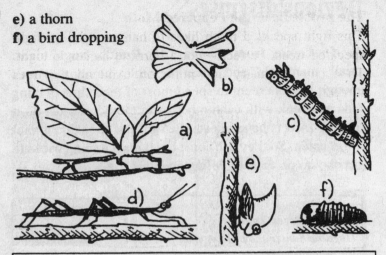

Tactic number 2: Blend in with your surroundings

Look like your surroundings, stay still, and the hunter might just miss you. The clear-winged butterfly, for example, is invisible – it has see-through wings that make it almost impossible to spot. But you may not be such a lucky bug. You wouldn't want to be a poor old peppered moth for example...

116

The problems of the Peppered Moth

This light speckled moth likes to hang around on light speckled trees. Perfect – not a horrible hunter in sight. Then came industry and pollution. And all the trees turned black.

BEFORE   AFTER

Suddenly the moths stood out like sore thumbs. The birds had a bonanza munching millions of moths. But some moths survived – only the ones with very dark colouring, though.

For years these dark moths had had it tough, trying not to be noticed on all those light speckled trees. Suddenly they had a bright future hiding on dark sooty ones. Or they did – until the cities started getting cleaner and the trees started getting lighter again!

Tactic number 3: Brilliant bluffs
Disguise yourself as a dangerous character and you can

bluff your way out of danger.

1 Hover-flies are harmless little things. An ideal dish for an ugly bug's dinner. Or they would be if they weren't wickedly disguised as wasps! Clear-wing moths try the same trick too, but they're even better bluffers – they can make the sound effects, too!

2 Ladybirds taste terrible. On the other hand, fungus beetles taste quite nice (if you're another insect, that is). That's why fungus beetles go around pretending to be ladybirds.

3 Some butterflies even disguise themselves as other types of butterfly. In South America there are four strangely similar-looking varieties of butterfly. Only *one* is nasty to eat. The other three are just plain copy-cats.

4 Another great little bluffer is the hawk moth caterpillar. Its head looks fairly normal, for a caterpillar – but it's rear end looks more like a snake's head!
But, beware of disguises...

5 The African dead-leaf cricket is cleverly disguised to look just like any rotten old leaf. It's got one little problem. The casque-headed frog also looks like a rotten old leaf – and this rotten old leaf likes nothing better than a cricket for its tea.

6 Best bluffer of all has to be the puss moth caterpillar.

Take a look at its ugly mug! Would you want to meet that on a dark and stormy night? You'd do well to avoid this little cruel cat, as it can spit out its half-digested dinner mixed with awful acid.

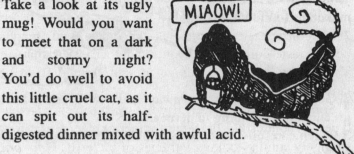

Tactic number 4: Horrible hiding places
One sure way to avoid being eaten is to hide somewhere horrible. That way no one can find you and no-one would want to either!

For example, the plume-moth caterpillar hides out in the sundew plant. The sundew plant eats flying insects, but the caterpillar is safe inside the plant and it gets to drink the droplets of sundew goo and munch on the sundew's insect tea.

Froghoppers hide inside a mass of foam. It looks a bit like bubble bath, but they make it themselves. The foam stops froghoppers from drying out in the sun, and it has a revolting flavour to put off horrible hunters.

Dare you make friends with ... a froghopper?

1 Look for its little drops of foam on the long grass in early spring. The foam is sometimes called "cuckoo spit" – you can guess why!

2 Gently brush the foam away and you'll see a little greenish insect hiding underneath.

3 Watch carefully as it blows bubbles from the end of its body to cover itself up again. The froghopper sucks plant juices and mixes them up with its own natural bubble-maker to make the froth.

OK, so maybe the froghopper doesn't want to make friends, but your've got to admit it's got a devilish disguise.

Ugly bugs vs horrible humans

Since the day that a caveman or cavewoman first squashed a cockroach there has been a non-stop war between ugly bugs and humans. It's the biggest war the world has ever known.

You might think that humans have an advantage over insects. A human is far bigger than the biggest insect. So humans can easily squash the insect. Humans are more intelligent than insects. (Well, *most* humans are!) But if you look at what humans and insects can do for their size the picture is very different.

Ugly bug olympics
Running *Winner:* One species of cockroach can run 50 times its body length in one second. *Loser:* The fastest human to run 50 times his own body length (about 80 metres) was about ten times slower.

The high jump *Winner:* Fleas can jump 30 cm (12 inches) – that's 130 times their own height. *Loser:* To match that a human would have to jump 250 metres (273 yards) into the air!

The long jump *Winner:* Jumping spiders can leap 40 times their body length. *Runner-up:* Grasshoppers can leap 20 times their own body length. *Loser:* To match that a human would have to leap the length of nine London buses in a single jump!

Weight-lifting *Winner:* Scarab beetles can lift weights 850 times heavier than their own bodies. *Loser:* To equal that a human would have to lift eight London buses at the same time!

Walking on the ceiling *Winner:* Flies. *Loser:* Humans can't do this at all.

Surely though, we humans are better at some things. Like building for example. I mean – there's the pyramids and St. Paul's Cathedral and the Taj Mahal. Ugly Bugs can't match that ... can they?

Bet you never knew!
Termites build gigantic nests. One nest contained 11,750 tonnes of sand. The termites had piled it up grain by grain and stuck it all together with spit! Beat that – humans!

But who are the dirtiest, the greediest and the most destructive creatures on the planet – ugly bugs or horrible humans? You might find it difficult to choose between them.

Filthy Flies

They never give up. It doesn't matter how many times you let them out the window, they always come back.

1 Blowflies enjoy eating rotting meat and animal droppings. They lay eggs on rotting meat and even do terrible things to your Sunday roast.

ROAST CHICKEN – ALMOST AS TASTY AS CHICKEN DROPPINGS!

2 The common housefly has common table manners. It drops in for dinner uninvited and sicks up over its food. And then it's been known to serve up a free selection of over 30 deadly diseases.

Horrible Humans

Humans are also very persistent. Once they decide to do something they will do it even if it costs the Earth – literally.

1 Humans are the only animals that deliberately destroy their environment. Every second humans devastate a hectare of forests, grasslands or swamps to build things for themselves. Each year humans burn an area of rain forest the size of Great Britain.

2 Humans also pollute the world with litter and dangerous chemicals. Every day humans dump 26 billion tonnes (27 billion tons) of rubbish into the sea.

3 Human beings are killers. Every hour of the day human destruction and pollution of the environment wipes out an entire species of living plant or animal.

Horrible humans hit back

Day after day humans wage war against insects with every weapon at their disposal. But they've also discovered some surprisingly horrible uses for insects and other ugly bugs.

Revolting recipes

If you can't dispose of ugly bugs you could always eat them. That's what millions of apparently sane people do throughout the world. Would you want to try any of these dishes?

Starters

Fried and salted termites

An African treat. Tastes like fried pork rind, peanuts and potato chips all mixed up!

L'escargots

Oui, mes amis! The traditional French delicacy. (Snails to you.) Fed on lettuce. Boiled and cooked with garlic, butter, shallots, salt, pepper and lemon juice. Served with parsley. Bon appetit!

Fried witchetty grub

A native Australian delicacy – these are giant wood-moth grubs. They look a bit like fusilli pasta and swell up when fried. Delicious!

Main courses

Stir-fried silkworm pupae

This tasty traditional Chinese dish is prepared with garlic, ginger, pepper and soy sauce. Wonderful warm nutty custard flavour. You spit out the shells. Very good for high blood pressure.

Roast longhorn timber beetle

Deliciously crunchy balsawood flavour. As cooked by the native people of South America.

Fried Moroccan grasshopper

Boiled bug bodies prepared with pepper, salt and chopped parsley then fried in batter with a little vinegar. You can also eat them raw.

Blue-legged tarantula

A popular spider dish in Laos in South-east Asia. Freshly toasted and served with salt or chillies. Flavour similar to the marrow in chicken bones.

Sweets

Mexican honeypot ants
A sweet sticky treat.

Baked bee and wasp grubs
An old recipe from Somerset in England. Juicy grubs baked in hot sticky honeycomb.

After your meal
Try one of our tarantula-fang toothpicks as used by the Piaroa people of Venezuela.

Ugly bugs v. horrible humans: the debate

For every argument there are two points of view. And this is certainly true for ugly bugs and humans. See for yourself. Who do you sympathise with most – ugly bugs or humans?

Human point of view	Ugly bug point of view
Ugly bugs sting and bite us.	Humans trap us, poison us and experiment on us.
Ugly bugs eat our crops.	Humans destroy our food plants and plant their crops too close together so we've got nothing else to eat.
Ugly bugs creep into our homes.	Humans destroy our homes.
Ugly bugs spread diseases.	Humans spread pollution and rubbish.
Ugly bugs destroy our furniture.	To us it's only wood.
Ugly bugs cost us money.	Who cares about money?
They destroy our property.	Who cares about property?

Ugly bugs just want the same things we want. Nice food and somewhere to live. The problem only comes when their idea of nice food is *your* nice food, and their idea of somewhere to live is *your* bedroom.

The ugly truth

You might think that humans are the deadliest enemies of ugly bugs. Wrong. The deadliest enemies of ugly bugs are other ugly bugs. Without ladybirds we'd be overrun by aphids. Without spiders we'd be fighting off flies.

The best way to remove an ugly bug is to get another ugly bug to do the job. When the cottony-cushion scale insect invaded California it finished off entire fruit crops. Until humans brought in a type of ladybird to crush the cottony crooks.

And remember all those scary statistics about insects having millions of offspring? You'll be reassured to know that the weight of insects eaten by spiders in a year is greater than the combined weight of all the people on earth. And if ugly bugs really *were* our enemies do you think we'd stand a chance? Nope. Quite apart from the fact that there's a million of them to every one of us – they can do horribly ugly things that we wouldn't even want to dream about.

But there's another side to ugly bugs. All ugly bugs are horribly incredible. Horribly interesting. And amazingly enough some ugly bugs are even horribly useful to humans.

We rely on ugly bugs to make plants fruit and to eat up rotten plant rubbish. Without insects we'd have no honey and no firefly lanterns. No silk, no jewel beetles and no beautiful butterflies. Admittedly we wouldn't have plagues and half-nibbled vegetables either. Ugly bugs make the world a worse place. But they make the world a better place too. And that's the Ugly Truth!

NASTY NATURE

Introduction

Brute force. Beastly behaviour. Animal cunning. Whenever humans have anything nasty to say to one another they drag animals into it. And animals bring out the worst in some humans, which can lead to nasty situations. . .

The science of animals can also provide some nasty surprises (and we're not talking about your brutish, wolfish, slavering teacher here). What, for example, about the odd words scientists use to describe our four-legged friends? They certainly leave a nasty taste in your mouth – when you don't understand them.

*ENGLISH TRANSLATION: COR – WHAT A NICE MOGGIE!

This is rather a pity because it's the nasty side of animals that give them their horrible fascination. Obviously, we're not talking warm and cuddly here. You might be pleased to wake up and find a fluffy kitten or a playful puppy on your bed. But what about a giant green toad with staring eyes and a warty skin? Or a sociable skunk or even a grinning gila monster with huge claws?

Yep. Some creatures are cold and slimy with gigantic teeth. Others like to suck blood and live in horrible places. In a word – they're NASTY. And oddly enough that's what this book is about. Nasty Nature. The sort of things that 99 per cent of teachers wouldn't dream of teaching in their worst nightmares.

But who knows? After you've read up on reptiles and mugged up on mammals you could persuade your teacher that you're a "natural" scientist. Perhaps you might even discover a new kind of nasty creature. Or feel inspired to keep a new pet. . .

Don't worry it's not hungry . . . yet.

One thing's for sure. Science will never seem the same again!

Freaky creatures

Sometimes it takes a difficult person to crack a really difficult problem. And 300 years ago, scientists had an appallingly difficult problem. Explorers kept discovering freaky new kinds of animals – but how should scientists go about listing this huge variety of new creatures? It was a toughie.

Horrible Science Hall of Fame:

Carl Linnaeus* (1707-1778) Nationality: Swedish
(* This was his name in Latin – his real name was Von Linné.)

Carl Linnaeus was a difficult man. It wasn't simply that he was an inspired genius with an incredible memory. The trouble was that he knew he was, and he wanted everyone else to know, too. If anyone criticized him he turned nasty. He sulked like a spoilt child and he never admitted he was wrong – never, ever, ever. Not even when he made big mistakes, like claiming a hippopotamus was a kind of rat!

HIFFOFOTAMUS

BLIMY – MY CAT CAUGHT ONE OF THOSE LAST NIGHT!

To be fair to Carl he'd seen rats before but not hippos.

But when Carl gave lectures, hundreds of students flocked to hear him. Why? Because he also told jokes. (A scientist with a sense of humour – now there's a rarity.)

Carl's quest

Carl Linnaeus had itchy feet – that's to say he never stopped moving around . . . and working. He travelled 7,499 km (4,600 miles) across northern Scandinavia and discovered 100 plants that were unknown to science. But his main aim was far more ambitious. This was to sort out all the plants and all the animals in the world into some kind of logical order.

Unfortunately, he liked some animals more than others. He had particularly nasty things to say about amphibia – that's creatures such as frogs and toads that live on land and in water. . .

Most amphibia are abhorrent because of their cold bodies, pale colour, cartilaginous* skeletons, filthy skin, fierce aspect, calculating eye, offensive smell, harsh voice, squalid habitation and terrible venom . . .

*from cartilage = gristle

Carl had his work cut out. There's an enormous variety of animals in the world. And thousands more were being discovered every year in unlikely places.

Bet you never knew!
There are currently about 10,000,000,000,000,000, 000,000,000,000,000,000 (that's 10 billion, trillion, trillion) animals on Earth (give or take a few million) and they come in all shapes and sizes.

Not a bad sort. . .

So how did Linnaeus sort 'em all out? He said that every type of animal was a species. Take this rather ugly toad.

NO THANKS

But following Linnaeus' plan, scientists call the toad a *Bufo bufo* – *bufo* is the name of the species and *Bufo* is the name of the genus it belongs to. (A genus is a group of similar species.) In fact, Bufo means "toad" in Latin, so the scientific name actually means "Toad toad".

Linnaeus placed each genus into a larger category called a family and grouped the families into classes. (Nothing to do with school you'll be relieved to know!) Our toad belongs to the family *Bufonidae* (Boo-fo-nid-ay) which includes toads and frogs, and the class Amphibia which also includes their slimy relatives, the salamanders and newts.

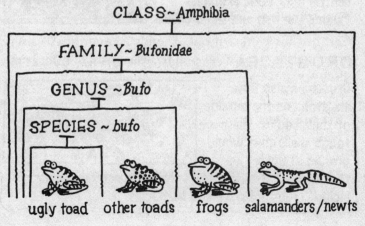

CLASS ~ Amphibia

FAMILY ~ Bufonidae

GENUS ~ Bufo

SPECIES ~ bufo

ugly toad   other toads   frogs   salamanders/newts

137

Gradually scientists throughout the world came to accept Linnaeus' methods of classification and they're still in use today. Here are the main animal classes. Now where do you fit in?

COELENTERATES (co-len-ter-ates) - 9,000 species

No, these aren't sci-fi aliens - they just look that way. They live in the sea and their bodies consist of a sort of stomach with tentacles armed with thousands of stinging cells. Nasty examples include jellyfish, sea anemones and corals.

ECHINODERMS (eck-hi-no-derms) - 5,000 species

These freaky creatures also hang out in the sea. They have hard, often spiky skin. Their legs are hollow tubes arranged around a central area. Eerie examples include starfish and sea urchins.

CRUSTACEA (crus-taysh-she-a) - 42,000 species

Crustacea also have skeletons on the outside of their bodies. These are tough shells that would give an attacker toothache if it tried to bite them. Crunchy examples include crabs, lobsters and barnacles.

ARACHNIDS (arack-nids) - 35,000 species

The bad news: most of this class are spiders. Erk! The worse news: some are scorpions. Arachnids have their head and thorax (the middle bits) of their bodies joined together. They have 6-12 eyes, eight jointed legs, two pincers and two grasping claws - oh, and I nearly forgot - a nasty poisonous sting in their tails. Some like playing sneaky tricks on humans - like hiding in their shoes!

FISH - 21,000 species

Most fish have bony skeletons - so when you eat one you can end up with a face full of bones. Other fish such as sharks have gristly skeletons instead. Fish live in water (surprise, surprise) and take dissolved air from the water through the gills in the side of their heads. Most fish are covered in scales and use fins to swim. Well, they're better than water wings.

AMPHIBIA - 3,200 species

Amphibia are cold-blooded. That doesn't mean that they're pitiless and ruthless killers, although many are. No, "cold-blooded" means they heat up and cool down with their surroundings. They have four legs and their skin is thin and slimy. The name amphibia means "double-lives" in Greek. And frogs and toads do live a double-life.

Dr Frog and Mr Tadpole

1 The tadpole hatches from eggs and gobbles up its unlucky brothers and sisters.

2 But in a few weeks it develops into a very different looking but equally repulsive adult.

3 The adult frog doesn't eat its own kind but it does grab flies with its long, sticky tongue.

4 Most amphibia spend the winter buried in mud at the bottom of lakes and ponds.

REPTILES – 6,000 species

Reptiles are cold-blooded too, and covered in scales. They have small brains for their size and their legs stick out of the sides of their bodies so they have to crawl around. (Unless they're snakes who slither about instead.) Young reptiles are hatched from eggs. (Don't try eating them for breakfast though.)

BIRDS – 9,000 species

Birds have two legs, a pair of wings and a horny beak. (Bet you bought this book to find that out!) Their bodies are covered with feathers made from keratin – that's the same stuff as your fingernails. Young birds hatch from eggs laid by their mums. That's if the eggs don't get poached and guzzled for breakfast first.

141

MAMMALS – 4,500 species

Mammals are warm-blooded* and most of them live on land and can't fly. Baby mammals are born alive rather than as eggs and they are nourished on milk supplied by their mums. And guess what – we're mammals too. Yes, humans belong to this class.

*This means that their blood is kept warm because their body is covered with fur or fat to keep the cold out. It's not the same as being "hot-blooded" – that's when someone keeps losing their temper and getting into fights.

Nasty habitats

Animals are found everywhere you can imagine and a few places that you wouldn't want to. By the way, scientists call the place where an animal lives its "habitat". Animal habitats range from deserts and rainforests to coral reefs and stinking swamps.

Mountain yaks happily explore the Himalayan mountains of Tibet at heights above 5,486 metres (18,500 feet). And they find the freezing temperatures of -17°C (1.4°F) well, rather bracing actually. Red bears are said to climb even higher and that's how they get mistaken for the legendary yeti.

142

Animals also lurk in the depths of the oceans. When explorers Dr Jacques Piccard and Lt. Don Walsh reached the deepest part of the ocean – 10,911 metres (35,802 feet) – in 1960, the first thing they saw was . . . a fish. As Piccard said later:

Slowly, very slowly, this fish moved away from us, swimming half in the bottom ooze and disappeared into the black night, the eternal night which is its domain.

The explorers were gob-smacked. They thought the weight of water crushing down on the sea floor would squash any creature.

Little and large facts

The largest animal that has ever lived is the blue whale. This creature can grow to 33 metres (110 feet) long and weigh 80 tonnes (79 tons). That's 24 times the size of an elephant and even bigger than the biggest dinosaur. Inside the blue whale there are over 8,500 litres (15,000 pints) of blood protected by a layer of fat 61 cm (2 feet) thick. But here's a nasty thought: since 1900 human hunters have brought at least 364,000 of these stupendous creatures to a horrible end.

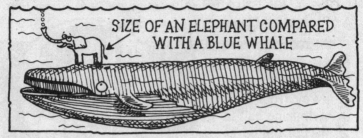

SIZE OF AN ELEPHANT COMPARED WITH A BLUE WHALE

Compare that with . . . Helena's humming bird. It's only 5.7 cm ($2\frac{1}{4}$ inches) from bill to tail and weighs a mere 2 grams (0.07 ounces). This tiny scrap of a creature lives off sweet, sticky nectar from flowers.

HUMMING BIRD

TUM TE TUM, DUM DI DOO DAH

BIRD HUMMING

The Marshall Islands goby is a tiddler of a fish that lives in the Pacific Ocean. It is only 1.27 cm ($\frac{1}{2}$ inch) long.

AH! A WORM!

ACTUAL SIZE

But there are some creatures that make a goby fish look like a blue whale. . .

Microbes fact file

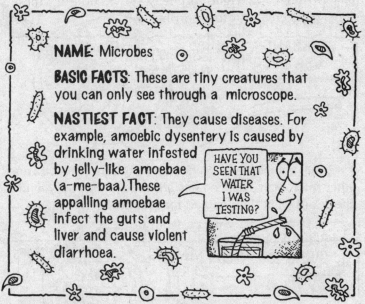

NAME: Microbes

BASIC FACTS: These are tiny creatures that you can only see through a microscope.

NASTIEST FACT: They cause diseases. For example, amoebic dysentery is caused by drinking water infested by jelly-like amoebae (a-me-baa). These appalling amoebae infect the guts and liver and cause violent diarrhoea.

HAVE YOU SEEN THAT WATER I WAS TESTING?

Millions of murderous microbes

A spoonful of soil can contain:

● 70,000,000,000 (70 billion) bacteria – these are tiny blobs of living matter that cause many diseases.

HAVE YOU SEEN MY BROTHER?

WHICH ONE? YOU'VE GOT 8 MILLION OF THEM

● 900,000 flagellata (flad-gell-la-ta) – these are microbes that swim using little whip-like tails.

● 42,000 amoebae – these feed by engulfing bacteria and other microbes. Their bodies are see-through so you can check out what they've had for breakfast.

● 560 ciliates (silly-ates) – these are creatures that use tiny hairs to swim about on damp lumps of soil.

Most of these creatures spend their time happily attacking and eating one another. And when they're not doing that they're pulling themselves in half to make even more murderous microbes. But these creatures aren't completely nasty. By feeding off dead plants and animals they ensure that useful chemicals are returned to the soil where they help make new plants grow. It's all in a good cause.

Bet you never knew!
In 1983 scientists discovered a super microbe lurking in a cavern in Arkansas, USA. It's a blob of jelly made up of millions of amoebae that slither along like a single creature! Its favourite food is bat droppings but it sometimes attacks lumps of fungus. It sends out fighter amoebaes to eat the fungus.

If you want to check out some seriously freaky creatures here are some examples. Which of these creatures is too strange to be true?

Weird wildlife quiz
1 The storsjoodjuret is an ugly looking long-necked reptile that skulks around in Lake Storsjön in Sweden. It's between 10-20 metres (32-65 feet) long. TRUE/FALSE
2 There's a type of bird with a horn on its head like a unicorn. It's called a "horned screamer". TRUE/FALSE
3 The Jack Dempsey fish is named after a famous American boxer. This small South American freshwater fish got its name because it enjoys ramming into other fish and stealing their eggs. TRUE/FALSE

147

4 There's a type of snake that can fly short distances. TRUE/FALSE

5 The Malaysian two-headed bat has a lump on its back that looks just like an extra head. This fools owls that attempt to bite the bat's head off in mid-air. TRUE/FALSE

6 The Indian climbing perch is a fish that climbs trees. TRUE/FALSE

7 The Iberian "singing" goat is an excellent mimic. (That's the posh name for someone who copies voices.) It has been known to imitate the yodelling calls of local mountaineers! TRUE/FALSE

8 There's a creature that hangs out in Australian rivers with a bill like a duck and fur like a beaver. It lays eggs like a bird and has poisonous spines like a lizard. TRUE/FALSE

Answers: 1 Probably FALSE although some people swear they've seen it. Maybe it's a relative of the more famous Loch Ness Monster. The Swedish government has banned attempts to kill or capture the creature just in case it does exist. 2 TRUE. The horn is 15 cm (6 inches) long. The bird itself lives in marshes in tropical South America. You can hear its scream 3 km (2 miles) away. 3 TRUE. 4 TRUE. The golden tree snake can glide 46 metres (150 feet). The snake launches itself from a high branch and draws its underside in and pushes its body forward as it zooms through the air. 5 FALSE. 6 TRUE. It uses its fins to grab branches. Once in the trees it allows ants to crawl over its body. Then it leaps back in the river. The ants fall off the fish and float around in the water – to be gobbled at leisure! 7 FALSE. 8 TRUE. It's the duck-billed platypus! This strange creature is actually an unusual species of mammal that looks like a mole pretending to be a duck. The puzzling platypus has also got detectors that sense electrical waves given off by small creatures at the bottom of muddy rivers. Classifying this freaky creature could drive a naturalist quackers.

Nasty naturalists

Naturalists are scientists who study the natural world. Some study particular animals and others look at an entire habitat and its wildlife. Mind you, some naturalists have nasty habits. Here's a particularly eccentric example:

Horrible Science Hall of Fame:

Charles Waterton (1782-1865) Nationality: British

Charles Waterton enjoyed pretending to be a mad dog and biting his visitors' ankles. A harmless youthful prank you might think, but cranky Chas was still playing this trick at the age of 57! Another curious habit was that he hated sleeping in a bed. He preferred a bare floor with a nice comfy block of wood for a pillow.

He made several trips to South America to find new types of animals – and then shot them. He stuffed their bodies so that he could study them at leisure. (He once captured an alligator alive by wrestling with it.) When at last he returned to his estate in England he spent £10,000 turning it into the world's first nature reserve. Yes, Waterton really liked animals – he even had his stables rebuilt so that the horses could "talk" to one another.

Now you might think Waterton was barking mad – horses don't talk, do they? Animals are not nearly as clever as humans (including naturalists and teachers) or are they? Find out in the next chapter.

Dumb animals?

So just how brainy are animals? And how good are their senses compared with our own? No one likes the idea that an animal might be brainier than themselves. That's why generations of nasty teachers have sunk to the depths of sarcasm.

YOU HAVE THE BRAIN OF A BIRD WILKINS, WHAT DO YOU SAY TO THAT?

TWEET, TWEET?

But would things seem so bad if your maths teacher had said "You have the brains of a horse"? Decide now as you read the story of. . .

Clever Hans

Berlin, Germany, 1904

The crowd was waiting, expectant. There was a buzz of excited conversation. Tired of standing, old Frau Schmidt turned to her younger friend, Fraulein Stein and whispered, "He's not going to appear!"

"'Course, he is!" said Fraulein Stein. "Just you wait. He always comes out at this time. And it's true what they say – he counts. That's why they call him 'Clever Hans'."

"How can that be?" asked Frau Schmidt suspiciously. "Horses can't count like humans – not in real-life, I mean."

"This one does – and better. They say that Wilhelm Von Osten – that's its owner, was a school teacher. When he retired he started teaching horses instead of children."

"Go on with you! What would he want to do that for?"

"He reckons horses are just as clever as children and easier to teach too. He even built a special classroom for horses. Mind you, they say Wilhelm used to shout at Hans when he made a mistake. Even used a whip."

Frau Schmidt cackled like an ancient hen. "My old teacher was a bit like that, too."

"Sssh!" snapped the man behind them.

They watched as Hans was led out into the courtyard. People craned their necks for a better look and there were cries of admiration.

"Ooh, isn't he beautiful," whispered Frau Schmidt to her friend. "Who are those people with him?"

"Top level big-wigs. Von Osten wrote to the government asking them to test the horse and prove his powers. So the government set up a committee." The women watched as a man set up something looking suspiciously like a school blackboard.

"Are we ready?" Professor Carl Stumpf asked his committee of experts.

"I still think it's a circus trick," said the circus trainer.

"The horse appears to be healthy enough for the test," said the vet cautiously.

"Hurry up – I'm late for a meeting," said the Very Important Politician looking at his silver pocket watch.

Wilhelm Von Osten was a severe-looking little man with a pointed moustache. But now he looked rather worried. This was the biggest test so far. Would Hans fail?

"Perhaps you'd like to think of a sum for the horse to attempt?" Professor Stumpf asked the politician.

"Humph," said that gentleman pompously. "Well, let me see. What about two times fourteen?"

Von Osten gripped a piece of chalk tightly in his hand and wrote on the blackboard, 2 x 14 = ?

The teacher bowed his head. "Now, Hans," he whispered anxiously, "I've got a nice juicy carrot for you. But you've got to get this sum right."

The courtyard fell silent. Hans gazed steadily at the board. After a few moments he tapped his left hoof twice.

"What's he doing now?" hissed Frau Schmidt.

"He's counting," whispered Fraulein Stein. "Left hoof means tens and right hoof means ones." Hans slowly beat his right hoof on the cobbles. By now everyone was counting the hollow beats. Clop, clop, clop, clop, clop. Hans stopped with his hoof in mid-air. He looked like a wooden horse on a merry-go-round.

"That's only five," announced the politician smugly. "I want it written down – the horse is an imbecile!"

Von Osten gripped the carrot until his knuckles turned white. But Hans hadn't finished.

Clop, clop . . . . and then finally . . . clop.

Hans looked at his master and whinnied happily. He knew he was right. The crowd clapped excitedly and a few began to cheer.

The politician's mouth dropped open like a trap door. Von Osten sighed with relief and gave Hans the carrot.

"Is that the right answer?" the circus trainer asked the vet.

"Yes, it is."

"That's incredible," said the trainer, scratching his head. "In all my years under the big top I've never seen anything like it."

"Nor I, in all my years in veterinary medicine."

"I told you so," announced Von Osten proudly.

Professor Stumpf asked the politician for his opinion.

The big, smug man had turned scarlet and was mopping his brow with a huge spotted handkerchief.

"Officially I couldn't possibly comment – but off the record I think I can say that I am . . . astounded."

He had quite forgotten his meeting.

But was Clever Hans really that clever? What do you think?

a) Von Osten was a ruthless trickster. He trained Hans to tap his hoof even though the horse didn't understand the questions.

b) Hans *was* clever. Since then scientists have proved that horses are better at maths than some humans.

c) Von Osten was giving clues to Hans. It wasn't the teacher's fault. He didn't know he was doing it.

Answer: c) This was proved by a young scientist Oskar Pfungst in 1907. He blindfolded Hans and found that the horse couldn't answer any questions. But if you think about it Hans *was* clever. He had realized that his teacher leant forward to ask him a question and straightened up when he gave the right answer. This is a useful tip for dealing with any teacher's questions.

Test your teacher

So how does your teacher measure up against the best and brightest of the animal world? Can he or she decide how clever these animals really are?

1 In the 1960s Dr Dorothy Megallon of Kentucky, USA ordered a specially designed car for her horse. She then tried to teach the horse to drive. What do you think happened?

a) The horse couldn't get started.

b) The horse drove perfectly.

c) The horse crashed soon after getting a ticket for speeding.

2 Gorillas at Frankfurt Zoo, Germany enjoy watching TV. What's their favourite viewing?

a) Soap operas

b) Wildlife documentaries about other gorillas.

c) Sports programmes including the football results.

THE GIRAFFES SAY "CAN YOU VIDEO IT FOR THEM, PLEASE?"

3 In 1913 a Mrs Moekel of Frankfurt, Germany owned a dog who could solve maths questions by moving beads on an abacus – a type of counting frame. But how smart was the dog?

a) Stupid wasn't the word for him. He only knew his two times table up to 4 x 2 = 9 (or was it 8?).

b) The scientists found that the dog had been trained to do certain sums but had no mathematical understanding.

c) The dog could work out square roots and was smart enough to help Mrs Moekel's children with their maths homework.

4 Keepers at San Diego Zoo, California, USA taught an Indian elephant to paint by holding a brush in her trunk.

How good were these pictures?

a) They were masterpieces as good as some modern art. Copies now hang in the world's major art galleries.

b) They were terrible – just a load of pointless scribble. Mind you, some critics have hailed them as triumphs of "post-modernist expressionism".

c) They were recognizable pictures, but since the keepers were telling the elephant what to do, they didn't count as the elephant's own work.

5 Scientists tested a chimp's intelligence by putting a blob of paint on its face and hanging a mirror in its room. The aim of the test was to see if the chimp realized the paint was on its face. What did the chimp do?

a) Looked in the mirror rather crossly and started rubbing the paint off its face.

b) Made faces at the mirror.

c) Tried to rub paint off the mirror.

6 British scientist Dr John Krebs added harmless amounts of a radioactive chemical to seeds and left them for marsh tits to hide and eat later. Then he used a Geiger counter (a machine that detects radio-activity) to monitor the hidden seeds. What did he discover?

a) Birds are brainy. The marsh tits cleverly hid hundreds of seeds every day. *And what's more, they were able to remember where they all were.*

b) Bird-brained wasn't the word for them. The birds soon forgot where they had hidden the seeds.

c) Nothing. The experiment was called off after the scientist forgot where he'd left his Geiger counter.

7 A scientist decided to teach three octopuses to pull a light lever in their tank in return for a feed of fish. What happened?

a) The octopuses were too stupid to learn the simple trick.

b) The octopuses turned nasty and tried to strangle the scientist with their disgusting long tentacles.

c) They quickly learnt the trick but after a few days they became bored and went on strike.

Answers: 1b) The car had levers to control its movement and an accelerator pedal that the horse could step on. The horse operated the steering wheel with its muzzle. Mind you, the horse wasn't allowed out on the open road! 2 c) Obviously they thought that the games were the real monkey business! 3c) Amazing but true. The dog, a three-year-old Airedale terrier named Rolf, was tested by a group of scientists who found that his abilities were real. Could you do with a pet like this? 4c) Elephants also draw "pictures" in the dust with their trunks but these really are meaningless scribbles. 5a) Chimps understand that the image they see in the mirror is their reflection. Monkeys do c) because they're not as smart as a chimp. How do you think your teacher would react first thing on a monday morning? 6a) But this is nothing. The North American nutcracker can hide up to 33,000 seeds – and find them again. 7c) They broke the light lever, squirted water at the scientist, and refused to take part in any more tests.

Bet you never knew!
Not all animals are clever. Some scientists reckon that the dumbest animal in the world is the turkey. Turkeys have been frightened to death by paper fluttering in the wind. Other turkeys have met nasty ends by cold or drowning because they're too stupid to shelter from the weather.

YES, BUT IF WE GO INTO OUR SHELTER, HOW WILL WE KNOW WHEN IT'S STOPPED RAINING?

Furry friend's feelings

For many years scientists believed animals didn't have feelings such as fear, anger and pride. But more recently they have begun to study this intriguing topic and they've come up with some freaky results. For example, baby elephants suffer from nightmares. Babies who have seen their parents killed by hunters wake up in the night crying. When they grow up these elephants sometimes attack humans as if seeking revenge. Is it because they "never forget"?

It's also said that elephants cry. There's a story that a circus elephant burst into tears after being hit by her cruel trainer. But boring old scientists point out that elephant's eyes water a lot anyway. Crocodiles weep too but for them it's a way of getting rid of unwanted salt. That's why we'll say someone's crying "crocodile tears" when they're just pretending to be sad.

Animals can feel happy. Gorillas supposedly sing when they're in a good mood. A singing gorilla sounds like a whining dog so it won't cheer up anyone else. Goats dance around and leap for joy when they're feeling chuffed. Perhaps instead of saying "happy bunny" we should say "happy goat" instead?

So it's official – animals are sensitive. But even if they didn't have feelings, they'd still be sensitive because animals have some pretty incredible senses. Which they need to survive in their favourite habitats. But how do they measure up to humans? Surely they couldn't compete?

STUNNING SENSE STATISTICS

ANIMAL SENSES 	HUMAN SENSES
SUPERSNIFFERS When you walk about in bare feet you leave 4 billionths of a gramme of sweat in each footprint. To a dog this stinks like a cheesy old pair of socks that haven't been washed for a month.	**DON'T SMELL TOO WELL** A human's sense of smell is one million times weaker than a dog's.  EVEN THOUGH HIS NOSE IS TWICE AS BIG
EAGLE EYES A golden eagle can see a rabbit on the ground up to 3.2km (2 miles) away.	**A SIGHT FOR SORE EYES** Some humans trip over rabbits.
A NASTY TASTE IN THE MOUTH Ugly catfish that lurk at the bottom of South American rivers have 100,000 taste buds in their tongues. That's how they find food in the murky mud.	**TOTALLY TASTELESS** Humans only have 8,000 taste buds - that's half as many as a pig. (This may explain why pigs don't enjoy school dinners but some humans do.)

HEAR, HERE
1. A dog's ear has 17 muscles so it can turn in any direction.

2. The Californian leaf-nosed bat can hear the footsteps of insects.

HARD OF HEARING HUMANS
1. Humans only have nine ear muscles and most people can't even waggle theirs.

2. Can you?

NO!

A TOUCH OF MAGIC
Seals use their ultra-sensitive whiskers to pick up tiny movements in the water caused by another creature.

A TOUCHY SUBJECT
Human whiskers don't even twitch.

IT'S TRUE!

STRANGE SENSES
1. Animals can predict earthquakes. The German scientist Ernst Killian found that dogs howl several minutes before a quake strikes.

2. The American knife-fish produces an electric signal 300 times every second. This creates a force field around the animal. A disturbance in the field warns the fish there's another creature about.

SENSELESS
1. Weedy humans can't accurately predict earthquakes even using sophisticated scientific instruments.

2. Er . . .

OK, YOU WIN!

Dare YOU find out for yourself . . . how cats see in the dark?

What you need:
1 torch
1 cat
1 dark room

All you do is:
Allow the cat a few minutes to get used to the dark. Shine the torch in the cat's eyes. What do you notice?
a) The cat doesn't notice the light.
b) The cat's eyes reflect back the light.
c) The cat's eyes glow red like a vampire's.

* REMEMBER TO MOVE ANY BOWLS OF CAT FOOD FIRST

Answer: b) The cat has a layer of cells at the back of its eye that act like a mirror. These reflect light inside the eyeball and allow the cat to see better in the dark.

Horrible Science Hall of Fame:

Karl Von Frisch (1886-1982) Nationality: Austrian
Karl was the son of a wealthy Austrian professor. He spent his childhood living in an old mill that his father was doing up and making friends with the local wildlife. He grew up to be a famous naturalist who discovered

how bees pass on messages by doing little dances. Here's one of his nastiest investigations. Could you solve this problem as easily?

Could you be a naturalist?

Professor Otto Korner of Rostock University cut up fish and found that fish ears didn't work like human ears. So he reckoned fish were deaf. To prove his point he put some fish in a tank and whistled at them. The fish ignored him.

To finally prove his case Otto asked a famous singer to perform a private concert . . . for the fish. She bawled out her operatic arias at an ear-splitting pitch. But still the fish took no notice!

Karl Frisch took an interest in this research and did his own tests. Imagine you were Karl Von Fish er, sorry, Frisch. What do you think you'd discover?
a) There's no doubt about it – fish are deaf as posts.
b) Don't be daft. It just proves that fish don't like boring old classical music.
c) Fish can hear but they're only interested in sounds to do with important things like food.
Are you sure they can't hear?

Answer: c) Karl blindfolded an unfortunate catfish and whistled every time he put some food on its nose. The fish tossed the food into its mouth. One day Karl whistled but didn't add the food. The fish reacted to the whistle by tossing its head. This is the reaction known to scientists as a conditioned reflex. The fish heard the whistle and learnt that it meant feeding time.

Many beasts aren't dumb animals at all. But what would they say to us if they could talk? Well, animals CAN talk . . . in a manner of speaking.

166

Snarls, growls and howls

Most animals communicate with one another to pass on nasty warnings or to show they're friendly. But creatures such as parrots can talk just like humans. Scientists say they're just copying the sound of the human voice. The animals don't realize what they're saying. Or do they?

Can animals really talk?
Look at this example and then decide for yourself.

A big-mouthed bird
For 12 years after 1965, the National Cage and Aviary Bird Show award for Best Talking Parrot-like bird was won by an African Grey parrot named Prudle. He knew over 800 words and even made up sentences. This amazed scientists who believed that parrots only copy what humans say.

Who's a pretty boy then?

In 1980, Dr Irene Pepperburg of Purdu University, Indiana, USA published a report on her research with an African Grey parrot named Alex. This brainy bird could ask for things such as a piece of paper to clean his beak. He knew the names of colours and shapes and even told Dr P. that he felt miserable when he moulted (lost his feathers).

A sign of wisdom

In 1966, some American scientists tried to teach chimpanzees sign language for the deaf. One of the first apes to learn this was a female called Washoe.

One day one of the researchers told Washoe that he'd just seen a big black dog with sharp teeth that ate baby chimps. Then he asked Washoe if she'd like to go outside. "NO!" signed Washoe nervously. After that whenever the scientists wanted Washoe to go indoors they told her that they'd seen the dog!

Despite falling for this nasty trick, Washoe proved to be a quick learner. She became so good at sign language she could even make up her own words such as "drink-fruit" (melon) and "water-bird" (swan).

SHE SAYS "YOUR HEAD LOOKS LIKE A MELON".

Washoe gave birth to a baby but sadly the infant fell sick and died at an animal hospital. The scientists came to tell Washoe what had happened.

"Where's baby?" signed the chimp.

"Baby finished," replied one of the researchers.

The poor mother retreated into a corner and wouldn't "talk" to anyone for several days.

In 1979, Washoe adopted a baby chimp and began to teach him sign language. Well, as they say, it's good to talk. . .

SHE'S TELLING HIM THAT IF HE DOESN'T EAT HIS DINNER, SHE'LL GET THE BIG BLACK DOG

Speak for yourself

Of course, when animals talk to one another they don't speak in human language. They've got their own forms of communication which can be quite complicated. Could you learn them?

TEACH YOURSELF LANGUAGE GUIDES

Liven up your holiday by talking to the wildlife. Now you can learn how to do this in the privacy of your own home. With these handy guides!

WHALE LANGUAGE

Have a "whale" of a time as you learn to sing like a whale for up to 24 hours at a time. Learn to alter your song if you're addressing a female whale. Practise ultra-low noises that can be picked up by whales hundreds of kilometres away! Be careful, though, no one knows what these songs mean so let's hope the whales don't get too excited when you sing to them.

IMPORTANT WARNING

WHALES CAN SING UNDERWATER BY MAKING SOUNDS IN THE HOLLOW SPACES INSIDE THEIR HEADS. HUMANS CAN'T DO THIS, SO DON'T TRY TO SING UNDERWATER.

KILLER WHALE

HELP!

DOLPHIN LANGUAGE

Discover how to natter with your flippered friends.

SQUEAKY WHISTLE = I'M SCARED.
LOTS OF WHISTLES = I'M LONELY.
CHATTERING JAW = GO AWAY.
CLICKS = FOOD IS NEARBY.
SLAPS TAIL = NOW I'M REALLY CROSS.

DOLPHIN   SHARK

SQUEAKY WHISTLE, NOW LET ME SEE...

GORILLA LANGUAGE

Ever wanted to gossip with a gorilla?
Here's a few words of gorilla language
to get you going!

WRAAGH! = DANGER!

GRUNT = BEHAVE YOURSELF (USED BY ADULT
GORILLAS TOWARDS THEIR YOUNGSTERS.)

A BARKING HOOTING SOUND = I'M CURIOUS.

HOO, HOO, HOO = KEEP OUT!

BEATING CHEST = I'M BOSS.

HOO, HOO, HOO!

WRAAGH!

SPINY LOBSTER LANGUAGE

You'll need a comb and a finger for this one. Free comb with every
guide, but you'll have to use your own finger. Spiny lobsters rasp
their antennae against a sticking out part of their shells.

SLOW RASP — IT'S SAFE TO FEED

RAPID RASP — TAKE COVER, THERE'S A SHARK ABOUT!

WHO'S THIS
WEIRDO
TELLING ME
IT'S SAFE TO
FEED?

MANUFACTURERS' WARNING

TO AVOID NASTY SCENES DON'T
PRACTISE YOUR ANIMAL SOUND
EFFECTS AT FAMILY MEAL TIMES.
FARMYARD IMPRESSIONS ARE
ALSO STRICTLY FORBIDDEN!

OINK, OINK!

I WISH HE
WOULDN'T EAT
LIKE A PIG

> *Bet you never knew!*
>
> *Some of the loudest animal noises are made by South American howler monkeys. Their dawn cries warn other howler monkeys to keep off their rainforest territory. You can hear the howls 2 km (1.2 miles) away. Unfortunately, they can attract passing harpy eagles. The giant bird grabs an unsuspecting monkey in its claws and tears it to pieces.*

Could you be a naturalist?

Vervet monkeys in Kenya have different alarm calls for leopards, eagles and snakes. A naturalist played these calls to the monkeys. What do you think they did?

a) Stuck their fingers in their ears and ignored the sounds.

b) The monkeys acted as if these dangerous animals were approaching.

c) The monkeys pelted the tape recorder with rotten fruit.

Answer: b) Leopard alarm — monkeys climbed the trees. Eagle alarm — monkeys took cover under trees. Snake alarm — monkeys checked the bushes.

Colourful characters

Some animals communicate without saying a word or making a sound. (Certain adults think that children should be able to do this too!)

1 The tilia fish of the Indian Ocean turns dark grey when it wants a scrap. If it loses, the fish turns white – maybe it's scared!

2 When the male tilia fish fancies a female his head turns brown, his jaw turns white and his fins become blood red.

3 Some humans turn an interesting shade of beetroot when they're cross, but did you know that octopuses are similar? Only not so bad. An angry octopus turns a tasteful shade of pink.

4 Fiddler crabs turn red when they're cross, black when they're scared, and a rather fetching shade of purple when they meet a fiddler crab they fancy.

If you can't change colour, you can always tell people what you think by the look on your face. Birds, reptiles and fish can't make faces, but mammals can. We've all seen the nasty expression on a teacher's face. But did you know monkeys make faces too? Famous naturalist, Charles Darwin, studied these fascinating faces.

Horrible Science Hall of Fame:

Charles Darwin (1809-1882) Nationality: British

Charles Darwin nearly gave up science at an early age. At school scientific interests were not encouraged and young Charles once got told off for "wasting time" on chemistry experiments. He later wrote:

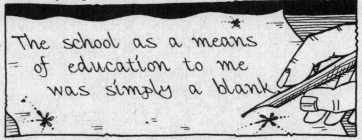

The school as a means of education to me was simply a blank

Try quoting that to your science teacher!

But Charles followed his scientific interests and in 1858 announced his "Theory of Evolution". Studies of fossil bones showed that ancient animals looked different from today's creatures. So the new theory arrived to explain these changes. Darwin suggested:

1 That some animals survive and some get guzzled. (Amazing insight, that.) Naturalists call this grisly business "survival of the fittest". Well, you have to be pretty fit to escape from a hungry tiger.

2 The animals in a species are all slightly different from one another. (You look different to the others in your class, don't you? I mean, even a teacher can tell you apart.)

YES SIMPKINS, IT IS TRUE THAT YOU LOOK SLIGHTLY DIFFERENT FROM OTHERS IN THE CLASS

3 Some animals in a species have features that give them a better chance of surviving. For example, take a bird like a nightjar. This bird is active at night and by day rests on the ground. Some nightjars are better camouflaged than the others. And you'll be glad to know they pass their crucial colouring on to their offspring.

4 After a while, you get more and more well-camouflaged nightjars because other nightjars are more easily spotted and scoffed by marauding cats.

5 This explains why after millions of years of evolution, each animal changes in appearance and ends up well-suited to its way of life. Either that, or dead.

At first, many people were appalled by Darwin's suggestion that humans had evolved from apes. But nowadays, Darwin's theory is accepted by many scientists as they continue to figure out how evolution operates.

FOR EXAMPLE, THE DODO DID NOT SURVIVE BECAUSE:
1. IT COULDN'T FLY
2. IT WAS EASY TO CATCH
3. IT TASTED NICE

Monkey business
London Zoo, 1850

The passers-by stared in horrified disbelief.

"Do you think he ought to be in there?" the young woman asked clutching the arm of the gentleman beside her.

"Assuredly not, my dear," he replied. "Such goings-on should be discouraged by the proper authorities."

An older man now joined them outside the monkey cage. "It's a disgrace," he snorted. "That Darwin should be arrested!"

Inside the cage Charles Darwin, the eminent naturalist, was down on all fours. He was making strange noises in a bid to make friends with a young orangutan. The ape was shrieking and leaping about with excitement.

Darwin tried blowing kisses at the ape. To everyone's amazement, including Darwin's, the orangutan suddenly blew a kiss back. Mr Darwin had made a new friend.

"Aha!" said Darwin to himself, still totally unaware he was being watched. "Very interesting!"

Pausing only to scribble illegible notes in his pocket book, the naturalist showed the ape a mirror. Once again the animal kissed the air with a loud smack of the lips. Then he peered behind the mirror hoping to find another orangutan. "That fooled you," laughed the naturalist.

By now the passers-by had scurried off with backward looks of disgust. But Darwin didn't mind. He'd proved that apes make faces to send messages and, as he was about to find out, we humans aren't so different.

Darwin then turned his attentions to his baby son, William. The naturalist took to creeping up on the infant and shaking a rattle loudly to startle him.

He found that babies don't learn how to smile and frown – they just know. This is called "instinct". So Darwin sent questionnaires to civil servants in other countries and found that people smile and frown all over the world in just the same way. These are natural ways for humans to communicate, whatever their language. This was a major discovery and it all began with a bit of monkey business.

Dare you find out for yourself . . . how to talk to an ape?

Here are some gestures you might find useful when you meet a monkey. You could practise them in front of a mirror (but not during a science lesson).

1 Kissing gesture:

Meaning: Help me please, I'm a friend.

Note: If a monkey makes this gesture it's a good idea to copy it. Hopefully you won't actually have to kiss the monkey.

2 Smacking lips:

Meaning: I love you and I want to eat the bits of dead skin and ticks in your hair.

Note: Monkeys do this to their friends. So if you smack lips to a monkey you better be serious about it.

3 Teeth chattering:

Meaning: HELP! I'm scared!

Note: Does anyone else have this effect on you?

Dare you find out for yourself . . . how to "talk" to your pet dog/cat?

If you don't happen to have a pet monkey, you may look out for these expressions on a pet dog or cat.

1 EXCITED EYES   Blinking eyes = I'm upset

2 FEARFUL FROWN

Frown. (Eyebrows lowered and eyes half-closed) = There's danger ahead

3 A CROSS CREATURE

Eyebrows down but eyes wide open = I don't like you. Note: It's always extremely rude to stare at a cat or dog. They get upset and if they happen to be much larger than you they might decide to take a chunk out of you.

4 EAGER EARS

Sideways ears = I'm resting

Twitching ears = I'm about to pounce.

Floppy ears =
I surrender!

5 MYSTERIOUS MOUTH

Mouth open but you can't
see teeth = Let's play

Mouth tightly closed =
I'm relaxed

Front teeth exposed =
I'm the boss.

All the teeth exposed =
You're the boss but I don't
like you and I'm going to
get you one day when I'm
feeling really brave.

IMPORTANT NOTE – You'd better "talk" nicely to your pet otherwise it might go wandering. You see, some animals have a nasty urge to drop everything and go on their travels.

Terrible travels

Just like humans, some animals enjoy travelling, and others prefer to stay put. But animals don't travel for fun or holidays. Oh, no. They're searching for food, for shelter or a mate. And some of their travels are definitely on the nasty side. Luckily some animals aren't too fussy about where they stay.

A nasty way to go

Just think of the nastiest, the hottest, the coldest or the WORST journey you've ever made. Now imagine making the same trip but with everything and everyone giant-sized, except you. And somewhere close by, large hungry creatures are waiting to pounce. . . Scared? That's how it feels to be a small animal on the move.

Yet amazingly, some animals make huge journeys – and can even find their way home from great distances with amazing accuracy. Impossible? How's this for a tall tail – er, tale?

Until 1952 headmaster Stacey Wood lived in California, USA. In that year he retired to a farm in Oklahoma – 3,000 km (1,875 miles) away. The whole family went except for the cat, Sugar, who was sent to live with neighbours. One year later a cat turned up at the Woods' new home. It was thin and bedraggled as if it had been on a long and desperate journey.

Amazingly, against all the odds, the new arrival was Sugar, who had disappeared a few weeks after the family had left California. The cat even had Sugar's bad hip. For an entire year the courageous cat had trekked across the United States to find its family. And to this day no one knows how Sugar did it.

Other animals are also brilliant at finding their way. Take pigeons, for example.

Pigeon power

Now you might think a pigeon is a silly-looking bird with a tiny little head and a puny little brain to match. And of course, you'd be right. But when it comes to travelling, pigeons and many other birds are geographical geniuses.

INCREDIBLE EYESIGHT

DIRECTION FINDING BRAIN

SUPERSONIC HEARING

AMAZING FLYING POWERS

BIG FAT FLUFFY CHEST

1 Pigeons can fly all day at speeds of 112 km per hour (70 mph) and cover 1,120 km (700 miles) and still not get tired.

2 Pigeons' brains contain magnetic crystals sensitive to the Earth's magnetic field. This allows a pigeon to know which direction is north and which direction is home. This was proved in the 1970s when a scientist tied a magnet to a pigeon's head. The magnet confused the pigeon's crystals and the poor pigeon got lost.

3 Like other birds that fly long distances, pigeons can recognize landmarks and use the position of the sun and the stars to work out directions. They can even see rays of sunlight when the sun is behind a cloud.

4 And if all that wasn't enough, pigeons have the ability to hear ultra low-pitched sounds too low for a human ear. For example, a pigeon can hear waves crashing on a beach hundreds of miles away. That's how they know the way to the seaside.

5 With all these amazing abilities you won't be surprised to hear that a homing pigeon that wins races is worth its weight in gold. One such bird, Emerald, was sold in 1988 for £77,000 and even her eggs were worth £2,400 each. Drop a few of those and you could make the world's most expensive omelette.

But pigeons are just one species of high-flying, long-distance travelling birds. Lots of birds migrate or travel from one area to another – every year. They do this because they have a powerful urge to fly off in a certain direction to find more food or a suitable nesting site. But scientists don't really understand how and why the birds manage it. Would you enjoy a holiday like this?

WING~IT HOLIDAYS

SWIFT TOURS

Air tours of sunny south-east Africa. Get away from the nasty British winter. Non-stop air flights with in-flight refreshments. Just catch yourself a few crunchy insects on the way. Exclusive washing facilities – just whiz through a thunderstorm. Note to passengers: the trip covers 19,200 km (12,000 miles) and we won't be landing at all. Not even to visit the toilet.

WANDERING ALBATROSS TOURS

Antarctica is the last unspoilt continent on Earth. Now you can fly around its beautiful coast in search of fish. Enjoy panoramic views and a lovely smooth ride. Your wandering albatross pilot can glide for six days without beating a wing. In-flight meals include mouth-watering raw fish – with that "just caught" taste.

ARCTIC TERN TOURS

A holiday with a difference. Good weather is guaranteed! Yes, you can be sure that every day will "tern" out nice again! Escape the northern winter blues by flying direct to sunny Antarctica where the days are warmest at this time of year. Then back to the Arctic in time for summer. Lovely fish suppers are available all the way too.

The nastiest animal journeys

Other animals, besides birds, also migrate. Their journeys are full of difficulties and dangers. Here's some of the nastiest examples. Would *you* want to tag along with this lot?

Ambling amphibia

Every year thousands of fearless frogs and not-so-timid toads return to the ponds where they hatched as tadpoles. They do this to mate and lay eggs. Unfortunately, they often try to hop across roads without looking and end up squashed by cars. Sometimes they get there only to find humans have drained their pond. In other places, however, naturalists have built tunnels under the roads so the wandering wildlife can cross safely.

Sociable snakes

Every year 20,000 red garter snakes slither 16 km (10 miles) from their summer homes in the marshes of Manitoba, Canada to their winter hideaways in sheltered rocky pits. After the winter they return to the marshes. Nothing too nasty about that – as long as you don't mind the sight of thousands of snakes. The snakes insist on taking short cuts through people's homes and often inspect their dinner tables.

Loony lemmings

Lemmings are small furry animals that happily scamper about in the Arctic snow. But every 3-4 years things get difficult. A rapid rise in lemming numbers means there isn't enough food to go round. So the lemmings form a huge army and attack anything in their way – including humans. They even do crazy things like trying to swim wide rivers. Where are they going? The lemmings don't know. There's an old story that lemmings leap off cliffs during these migrations – but it's not true. That would be too crazy – even for a lemming!

Terrible turtle treks

Every year green turtles swim to Ascension Island in the Atlantic Ocean to lay their eggs. No one knows why they go there but the island has few large animals that want to eat the turtles. Unfortunately the island is only 13 km by 9 km (8 by 5.6 miles) in size and some turtles have to swim 2,080 km (1,300 miles) to get there. To make matters worse the tired turtles' top speed is only 3 km (less than 2 miles) an hour.

A slippery trip

For fifteen years a European eel does nothing very much except squirm around in a muddy river or pond. Every so often it scrunches a passing fish and that's it for excitement. Then one day the eel starts feeling eel – er sorry, ill. It turns from yellow to silver and its eyes bulge.

Its snout gets longer and – eel-longated (ha ha). Then the eel develops an irresistible urge to swim to the sea. So strong is this feeling that an eel will even slither to the nearest river over dry land. The eel swims the length of the river to the sea and wriggles up to 4,000 km (2,500 miles) to the Sargasso Sea – a vast area of seaweed in the Atlantic Ocean.

When it gets there . . . the exhausted eel dies. Bit of a wasted effort you might think – except that just before it dies the eel mates. Its offspring (called elvers), tiny see-through eels, set off for home. Without any help they find their way to the rivers and ponds of Europe.

And guess what? No one knows how eels came to develop this amazing lifestyle or how they find their way on their mysterious migrations.

No matter how far it has to go, every animal's body is suited to getting around. That's why dolphins have flippers, birds have wings and frogs are champion hoppers. Here's your chance to get moving on this topic.

Dare YOU find out for yourself . . . how you measure up to a gibbon?

How good are you at brachiation (brach-ee-ay-shun)? If your answer is "my bike brakes are fine", you ought to know that brachiation means leaping from branch-to-branch. It's a dangerous way of getting to school in the morning. But gibbons brachiate all the time. That's not surprising, really – gibbons are apes that live in the trees of south-east Asia.

Here's the secret of their success:

GIBBON FOOT

HUMAN FOOT IN SOCK

DISGUSTING SMELL

Take a look at this gibbon's foot. Now compare it to your own right foot. (It helps if you take off your sock.) What do you notice?

a) Nothing. My foot is exactly the same.

b) The gibbon's big toe looks more like my thumb.

c) The gibbon's toes are longer.

Eventually, though – just like you at the end of a hard day in the classroom – every animal's thoughts turn to home. But for an animal "home" isn't a place to watch TV or play computer games. It's somewhere to store food, raise young and shelter from larger, fiercer creatures. Bet you wouldn't feel at home in any of these places.

Nasty home truths

1 The Australian white tree frog is a friendly little creature with a big smile on its slimy face. Clearly, this happy hopper is very pleased with its favourite home – a toilet cistern. (Before the invention of the toilet the frogs lived in smelly ponds.)

AAAAGH!
'THERE'S A
FROG
IN THE BOG!

2 Snapper turtles in eastern North America are quite at home in smelly stagnant ponds or stinking sewers. It's a bad idea to go paddling in these places (as if you would!). Snapper turtles lurk in the shallows and they'd love nice pink toes for tea.

3 An octopus will live in any hollow object lying on the sea bed. They're really not fussy – for a small octopus a human skull makes a cosy little home.

4 Eagles and ospreys build large, scruffy twig nests on top of trees. Unfortunately, they also build them on electricity pylons. Sometimes a bird touches a power line and you end up with Kentucky fried eagle.

5 Cave swiftlets are birds related to swifts that live, not surprisingly, in caves. Their nests are made from bits of plants glued together with . . . spit. Yes – swiftlet spit sets swift-ly (ha, ha!) to form a strong glue. And this is added to chicken and spices to make traditional Chinese bird's nest soup. Oddly enough swiftlets eat something similar. They feed their young on balls of insects glued together with tasty all-purpose spit. Yummmeee!

Of course, not all animals build their own homes. It's too much like hard work. Some move into other animal's homes instead. For example, North American black-tailed prairie dogs are squirrel-like creatures that dig a maze of tunnels to live in. Some of these tunnel systems are huge with up to fifty entrances. Soon unwelcome lodgers move in, these include owls, squirrels, salamanders, mice, black-footed ferrets and even the odd rattlesnake.

And that's not the only way that animals take advantage of one another. Some do nasty things like – eating their hosts alive, or slurping their blood. Yikes! Read on if you dare. . .

THE NEXT CHAPTER'S REALLY GRUESOME!

Nice and nasty: helpers and hangers on

When different animals get together, things happen. Nice things and nasty things. Some animals help one another and some animals are just harmless hangers on . . . but others try to help themselves at the expense of other creatures.

Animal aiders

The idea of animals doing one another good turns sounds odd – doesn't it? But it shouldn't. After all, we keep pet dogs and cats – or even pet toads and snakes. Pets keep us company, often show us affection and leave little puddles on the carpet. In return, we feed them and provide shelter. And other animals such as horses and sheepdogs work for us in return for more food and shelter. When animals help one another this is known as symbiosis (sim-by-o-sis).

THANKS FOR GETTING RID OF THESE HORRIBLE TICKS

THANKS FOR THE DINNER

THANKS FOR LETTING ME GET AWAY!

Bet you never knew!

Animals raised by humans sometimes keep pets. One of the apes taught to "speak" using sign language in America, was Koko the gorilla. Now Koko was happy living with researcher Dr "Penny" Patterson. But the gorilla had one wish. More than anything else – she wanted a kitten of her own. So in 1984 kind-hearted Dr Patterson gave her one.

Koko called her new pet "All Ball". She treated All Ball as her baby and even dressed it in cute little hats and scraps of material. Koko often tried to get the kitten to tickle her. (The gorilla enjoyed being tickled by her human friends.) And when the kitten was well-behaved Koko signed that it was a "soft good cat". Altogether now – Ahhhh. But if you like happy endings don't read the bit below.

Soon after, All Ball was run over and killed. Boo hoo! Poor Koko was heart-broken and nothing could cheer her up until Dr Patterson bought her another kitten.

Feathered friends

1 There's one little bird in Africa that's fond of beeswax and the juicy grubs that wriggle around in the sticky honeycomb. But how to get it – that's the problem. The honey is protected by thousands of bad-tempered bees.

So the bird calls to attract a passing honey badger. Then the bird flies towards the bees' nest.

The badger has learnt to follow the bird's signals. The bees can't sting the badger's thick skin as it claws open the nest. Meanwhile, the bird gobbles up any spare honeycomb.

And the name of this bird? The honeyguide bird, of course.

2 Another African bird, the ox pecker, rides on the backs of hippo, zebras and rhinos. The larger animals don't mind. The bird eats the flies that infest their backs. And it even warns of approaching humans.

If the larger animal takes no notice, the bird drums its beak against their head.

Home helpers

Some creatures help each other by providing homes in return for services rendered.

For most fish, getting mixed up in the poisonous tentacles of a Portuguese man-o-war jellyfish is something they wouldn't live to regret – because they wouldn't live much longer. But for one fish this is home. Nomeus (no-me-us) is a little fish that lives amongst the tentacles, protected from harm by its extra slimy skin. The fish keeps the tentacles nice and clean. When other fish try to catch Nomeus they fall victim to the jellyfish – and Nomeus gets to eat the leftovers.

In a cosy, sandy burrow at the bottom of the sea live a pair of oddly-matched housemates – Luther's goby fish and the blind shrimp. The shrimp dig their burrow and the goby guides his friend on feeding trips. The shrimp keeps his antenna on the fish's tail. If there's danger, goby wags his tail and the two friends run off home.

But helping each other and looking after one another isn't all that animals do. Some even clean one another. And there's a great choice of cleaners – if you don't mind being nibbled.

CREATURE COMFORTS SERVICES DIRECTORY

HEY FISH – D'YOU FANCY A WASH AND BRUSH UP?

Let your friendly cleaner Wrasse do the job for you. We'll nibble that nasty mould and fungus away and leave your scales as good as new! Speedy personal attention assured.

ALMOST FINISHED

"Cleaner Wrasse managed to serve a queue of 300 fish in a single session. Highly recommended."

A. Shark (Pacific Ocean)

WARNING!

To all customers of Cleaner Wrasse Services: BEWARE OF CHEAP IMITATIONS! Blenny fish try to copy Cleaner Wrasse. They've even copied the stripe on our bodies. But BEWARE! As soon as they get close they'll take a bite out of you and scarper!

GOBIES' GOUPER GOB-GROOMING SERVICES

Are you a gouper fish with bad breath? Special offer – let us clean out your mouth free of charge! We'll eat those nasty bits of rotten food and we won't leave you feeling down in the mouth.

CROCS – ARE LEECHES YOUR PROBLEM?

There's nothing that spoils a good meal more than leeches clinging to your gums and sucking your blood. But spur-winged plovers have the leeches licked. Just open your mouth and we'll eat them for you. Also free danger-warning service. If you hear us chirp – there's a large, fierce animal on the way, so you'd better jump in the river!

Could you be a naturalist?

In coral reefs, fish cleaning is done by shrimps from special areas known as "cleaning stations". A scientist removed all the shrimps from a cleaning station. Can you guess what happened next?

a) The fish started nibbling one another in a vain attempt to keep clean.

WHERE ARE THEY?

DON'T ASK ME, I'M A PRAWN

b) Nothing. The fish weren't bothered whether they were dirty or not.

c) The fish went away in search of another cleaning station.

Answer: c) The fish staged a mass walk-out. Or should that be a swim-out?

Pesky parasites

But not all creatures are helpful. Some couldn't be helpful in a month of Sundays. They're known as parasites – animals that don't hunt for food, but steal it in various horrible ways from other creatures. These parasites do their victims no favours at all. Which of these parasites would you least want to meet?

Frigate birds of Central America have an unusual method of getting a free lunch. They wait until another bird has caught a fish then chase their victim and force them to sick up their meal. The foul frigate bird then gulps the sick in mid-air. And if that isn't nasty enough, they also steal eggs and eat other birds' chicks – including baby frigate birds.

European cuckoos lay their eggs in other birds' nests. The cuckoo hatches and chucks the other fledglings out of the nest. The parents feed the cuckoo and don't even notice any difference. Not even when the cuckoo grows up to five times their size. (Would your parents notice if you were replaced by another creature?) As soon as it's fully-grown the cuckoo takes off for a lovely winter holiday in Africa. And guess what? It doesn't even say "thank you".

Sea lampreys have been described as "a yard of garden hosepipe that's been left out all winter". And that's putting it nicely. These foul fish have no mouth or teeth – just suckers and fangs, and they like nothing better than sucking the blood of other fish.

Want to know something really scary? There's something that lurks in the South American jungle that makes other parasites seem almost OK. Oh yes, this is much, much worse. D'you want to know what it is? Turn down the lights, close the shutters and draw close to the fire. Here's a tale to make your blood run cold!

What's eating you?

"I can remember it like it was yesterday." The old man smiled showing the gaps between his yellow teeth. The gaps made him hiss as he spoke. Like a snake.

"But when did it happen, grandpa?" asked the young boy with his eyes like saucers.

"It was in Brazil, back in 1927. We were there to study the wildlife and it was my first time in the jungle. I remember the strange sights and the smells – but do you know what I remember most? The nights. The humming insects and the croaking frogs in the dank, smelly swamps. The wet chill in the air. The big round moon hiding amongst the trees.

"We made camp mostly around nightfall. Well, it gets dark quickly in the jungle and we had to light a fire and put our tents up in good time. Old Dr Beebe's orders. That's William Beebe of the New York Zoological Society – our expedition leader. And Dr B. said we should always keep our feet inside the tents."

"Why did he say that, grandpa?"

"Well, because of the vampires, of course," hissed the old man.

"Vampires? Not real vampires like Count Dracula?" The boy's voice rose higher.

"Dracula wasn't no real vampire, Johnnie. He was a legend. But this is true. As true as I'm sitting here. Real live vampire bats."

The young boy gulped.

"*Bats!* And do they really bite people?" he stammered.

"Sure they do – and animals like cows and horses. Not dogs so much. Dogs can hear 'em coming. The bats flap down from the trees where they live – silent as ghosts.

They've got wings like old leather and huge ears to hear with. They creep along the ground to find your feet. Then they lick your toes to make sure they're nice and soft. And then they *bite* you!"

The boy looked over his shoulder nervously. "Do they really suck blood?"

"No, they lap it up like a cat laps milk. Or at least that's what Dr Beebe told us. He was always going on about bats."

"Well, it was soon after that I got a rude awakening. I was in a deep long sleep. Suddenly, I felt a sharp pain in my big toe like a needle. I shouted and then I was awake. Sweat streamed off me like a waterfall. It was dark but there was a moon and I saw a figure. Someone. Something."

"Wasn't it a bat?"

"No – it looked human. It scared the life out of me, I don't mind telling you. My heart was banging like a drum. I reached for the electric torch. My fingers felt like slippery fish. Somehow I switched on the light and what do you think I saw? Dr Beebe. He was crouching there with a bright sharp pin in his hand. 'Sorry to disturb you,

Jack,' he chuckles. 'Just trying a little test. I wanted to see if a vampire's bite would wake you.'

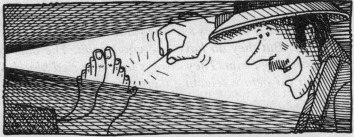

"Well, I was so shocked I just didn't know what to say. So I muttered something like, 'Looks like it just did.' And that was that. I got talking to some of the others the next day and it seems the doctor played the same trick on everyone. 'Practical research' he called it.

"Well, the following night I slept really well. Must have been the rude interruption the night before. When I woke up I felt fine. Until I looked at my feet and saw the blood. Those pesky vampire bats had come by – and I hadn't felt a thing!"

"Now then, Pa," said the woman. "Don't you go filling young Johnnie's head with moonshine. You know it's not true."

"Oh, but it is!" cried the old man sharply. He drew off his scuffed brown shoe and then a worn green sock. His foot was white and sinewy. Little blue veins criss-crossed the parchment coloured skin. Years after the event his toes were still pitted with white scars. Bite marks.

Mind you – there's one thing worse than being picked on by a blood-sucking bat. And that's having lunch with a horribly hungry hunter. Especially when it's YOU on the menu!

Horrible hunters

When you're hungry you probably pop out to the shops to buy food. It's called "shopping". Animals can't usually do this so, instead, they pop out and nab some unfortunate, small creature for their tea. Here's how they do it.

Horrible hunter types

Some hunters, such as lions and tigers eat large animals. For them life is rather relaxing. They spend most of their life sleeping off huge meals. They only hunt when they're really hungry. It helps to keep out of their way at these times. Other hunters such as wild dogs or hyenas will eat anything that comes along and they're always on the look out for a free lunch. Best avoid them at *all* times.

And beware. Hunters play horrible tricks.

Horrible hunter tricks

1 Sneak up on your victim. If they turn round freeze and pretend to be a twig. The olive green snake of Central America does this. It even sways in the breeze – before it strikes and grabs a poor little baby bird from its nest.

THEY HAVEN'T TWIGGED YET

2 The horned frog sits motionless except for one finger. This twitches until an insect or small creature comes by thinking it's something to eat. Big mistake. It's feeding time all right – feeding time for the frog.

3 There's a type of African mongoose with a bottom that looks like a small flower. The mongoose crouches on a shrub with its bum in the air. When an insect lands on the pretty "flower" the mongoose whips round and snaps it up.

4 White-coated polar bears are almost invisible against the Arctic snow. But the bear's large black nose is embarrassingly obvious when it sneaks up on a seal. So the bears push a lump of ice in front of them to hide their tell-tale noses.

5 Everyone knows that rattlesnakes have a rattle at the end of their tails. Some of their few fans say that the rattle is there to warn people to steer clear. Huh – as if snakes are that thoughtful. In fact, the rattle is there to distract attention away from the head with its fatal fangs.

Could you be as cunning as these horrible hunters? Now's your chance to find out. Imagine you were a lioness living on the plains of Southern Africa. What sort of a hunter would you make?

Lion hunting tips
The lionesses in a pride (group of lions) hunt together. (The lazy males don't take part.)

1 Your pride of lionesses stalk a herd of gazelles (small antelope). From what direction do you approach?
a) With the wind at your back so that the gazelles can smell you. This will scare them so much they won't be able to defend themselves.
b) With the wind blowing in your face so the gazelles can't smell you.
c) From the direction of the sun so that the gazelles are dazzled.

2 Your pride splits into two groups. What do you do next?
a) One group charges the gazelles and chases them towards the second group waiting in ambush.

b) One group goes after the gazelles and the others chase some nearby zebra. This doubles the chance of catching something.

c) One group chases gazelles and the others keep watch for marauding hyenas that might try to steal the meat.

3 You select a gazelle to attack. Which one do you choose?

a) The biggest – more meat for you.

b) The smallest – less likely to put up a fight.

c) The weakest – easier to catch.

4 The males invite themselves to the feast. While you and your sisters have been hunting the males have been lazing about in the sun. Now they're hungry. So who gets the lion's share?

a) The lionesses, followed by the cubs. The males are given a few scraps. Serves 'em right for not helping.

b) The males take the best bits. The lionesses and the cubs get what's left. If they're lucky.

c) The cubs. After all they need the food to help them grow.

5 A new male chases away the old males in your pride. He cruelly kills and eats your cubs. What do you do?
a) Run for the hills.
b) Kill him and eat his body.
c) Make friends with him.

6 In the dry season there's little food. What do you eat?
a) Other lions
b) Fish, insects, lizards, mice and the odd tortoise.
c) Bones buried for just such an emergency.

Answers: Give yourself one point for each correct answer. **1 b). 2 a)** Lions show a lot of teamwork when hunting. Some scientists believe that this is an illusion and all the lions are doing their own thing. **3 c). 4 b)** Males are bigger and stronger than the females. If there's not enough food for everyone the lionesses and cubs starve. **5 c)** Nasty but true. The male wants the lioness to look after his youngsters once they are born. The lioness wants the male to protect her from other males. **6 b)** A starving lion will eat anything so be careful if you're in the area.

What your score means:
5-6 A roar of approval. You'd make a great hunter.
3-4 You're mane-ly right but you need to lick your skills into shape.
1-2 You'll never be a lion. Best swallow your "pride" and stick to being a human.

Could you be a naturalist?

One fierce hunter from the African plains is the cheetah.

These big cats are the fastest creatures on Earth and reach speeds of 110 km an hour (69 mph) in short bursts. The problem is that a racing cheetah's muscles produce huge amounts of heat. If the cheetah ran at top speed for more than a few seconds it would suffer fatal brain damage. A puffed-out cheetah needs to put its paws up for a few minutes to recover.

In 1937 an animal collector staged races between a cheetah and a greyhound in London. What do you think happened?
a) The greyhound won.
b) The cheetah ate the greyhound.
c) The cheetah won but only sometimes. Most of the time she couldn't be bothered to make the effort.

Answer: c) Cheetahs don't like racing. In another race in 1937 a cheetah only completed half the course and then took a breather.

So far all the hunters we've been talking about have been land hunters. But that doesn't mean you'd be safe underwater – especially if you're edible. The seas and

211

rivers swarm with millions of ferocious fish. Which of these fish is too nasty to be true?

Far-fetched fish facts

1 A trumpet fish hitches a ride on a larger but harmless parrot fish. When the trumpet fish spots a small fish to eat it hops off to make a quick killing! TRUE/FALSE

2 Vicious blue fish attack schools of other fish off the Eastern coasts of North America. The brutal blues kill more than ten times the fish they can eat. They guzzle up to 40 at a time and then sick them up so they can go on eating! TRUE/FALSE

3 The halitosis haddock has a deadly and unusual weapon – its disgusting, smelly breath. When a smaller fish comes by, the horrible haddock breathes a cloud of poisonous bubbles to overwhelm its prey. TRUE/FALSE

4 The angler fish has its own fishing rod complete with a small worm-like object that dangles just above its mouth. When another fish comes to investigate the bait the angler fish snaps up its catch. TRUE/FALSE

5 The scissors fish has jaws just like a pair of scissors and it uses these fearsome weapons to slice up its prey. It's even been known to snip through the lines of deep sea anglers. TRUE/FALSE

6 The deep sea viper fish has 1,350 lights inside its mouth. They twinkle in the ocean depths and little fish flock to see the lovely spectacle. Once the fish are inside its mouth the viper fish closes its giant gob. End of show. TRUE/FALSE

Answers: 3, 5 FALSE. 1, 2, 4, 6 TRUE.

> **Bet you never knew!**
> *One fierce fish that's all too real is the great white shark. Did you know it senses movements in the water up to 1.6 km (1 mile) away? At 400 metres (440 yards) the shark can also sniff blood. It usually sneaks up behind or below its victim. At the last moment, the shark closes its cold black eyes and homes in on its victim's terrified heartbeat. Yes – the heartbeat produces tiny electrical waves and the shark senses these. Then it's GRAB-A-BITE time!*

Could you be a naturalist?

The archer fish of India, Australia and south-east Asia has an unusual secret weapon. A built-in water pistol. This 2cm long fish spits water with deadly accuracy at passing insects.

SORRY! I WAS AIMING FOR THE FLY

213

A public aquarium once kept a school of the fish and splatted 150 g (6 ounces) of raw meat on the sides of their tank. The owner wanted to see if the fish could dislodge the food. Could they?

a) These fish are little squirts. So they couldn't budge the meat.

b) The fish kept squirting until all the meat was in the water.

c) Unable to shift the meat by squirting the fish leapt up and grabbed it in their tiny jaws.

> **Answer: b)** Yes – they certainly made a big splash.

One of the fiercest hunters is one that you may have met already. Indeed this ferocious creature may be lurking behind your curtains or even watching your TV! Yes – we're talking about your not-so-cuddly cat. Here's where we let the cat out of the bag. Your pet leads a deadly double-life.

Tiddles the terrible

Tiddles rubs your legs. Just trying to be friendly? No way. She's leaving her scent on you to show you're part of HER family.

THAT'S MY GIRL

Tiddles has her own hunting territory. Normally she won't allow any other cat into this area. The territory is a little larger than your garden.

Tiddles hunts by sneaking up on prey. Sometimes she freezes before moving stealthily forward once more. At the last moment she pounces.

Tiddles enjoys catching insects. They have such a lovely crunchy texture – it's just like you eating crisps.

But she doesn't like catching rabbits or rats. She's scared of rabbits because they're so big. And she thinks that rats taste worse than cheap cat food.

When Tiddles "plays" with mice she's not being cruel. Oh no? She's just a big scaredy-cat. Scared the mouse will fight back (some mice do). So she keeps her distance without losing the mouse.

Tiddles eats mice head first. Gulp. Before eating birds she plucks out the feathers with her teeth.

1ST COURSE = MOUSE

2ND COURSE (ALREADY PREPARED) = BIRD

When Tiddles brings you a half-dead mouse or battered bird it's her way of teaching you to hunt. Yes – she wants you to finish it off. Mother cats do this to train their kittens.

ARRRGH!

MUST BE SOME SORT OF BATTLE CRY BEFORE HE JUMPS ON IT

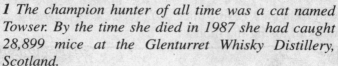

Bet you never knew!

1 The champion hunter of all time was a cat named Towser. By the time she died in 1987 she had caught 28,899 mice at the Glenturret Whisky Distillery, Scotland.

2 A cat's skill in hunting once saved a man's life. The man in question was Sir Henry Wyatt, a 15th-century English knight who was locked in a dungeon and left to starve. But hungry Henry was befriended by a stray cat. The cat brought in birds such as pigeons and kept the knight alive until he was released by friends.

Mind you, if cats have ambitions, it must be every cat's dream to be a really big cat. A really big cat and a really deadly hunter. Something like a tiger, in fact.

Terrible tigers

From its nose to the tip of its stripy tail the average tiger is 2.9 metres (9 feet 6 inches) and weighs 204 kg (32 stones) – that's the weight of three grown men. In the 19th century, Victorian writers gave the tiger a bad press. They saw the tiger as a treacherous enemy that took its victims by surprise. The Hon. James Inglis wrote:

... the tiger is ... a cunning, sneaking rogue ... a cruel, whiskered robber.

19th-century hunters enjoyed "bagging" tigers and they even got paid for their horrible pastime by the Indian government! Many tigers ended up as grisly tiger skin rugs. But the hunters were far too deadly for the tigers. By 1972 there were only about 1,800 tigers left alive in the whole of India. Hunting was banned in 1971 and thanks to a massive conservation effort, tiger numbers began to increase in some areas. But the naturalists' work raised a nasty dilemma. What should be done when a tiger attacks humans? Was it ever right to kill a tiger?

The tiger must die
India/Nepal border 1978

"The tiger must die. I could have shot it myself!" cried the Forest Park Director thumping his desk.

"You don't understand," said Arjan Singh the tiger expert. He was slightly built and balding and right now his brow was creased with worry.

The Director's mouth set in a hard line. He wiped the sweat off his fleshy face with a damp handkerchief. It was very hot, even though the blinds were drawn and the ceiling fan whirred lazily. "No, Mr Singh, it's you who doesn't understand. Let's review the facts, shall we? On

3 April a man disappeared in the forest. Tiger victim number one. What was left of him after the tiger had finished didn't even fill a shoe box. Three days later another man went missing. I saw the tiger eating his body. I shouted but the monster took no notice. I wish I'd shot the tiger then and there."

His finger curled round an imaginary gun trigger.

"But tigers are protected," said Arjan Singh, "you can't go around shooting them."

"Human beings must be protected too!" roared the Director. "Two men are dead and you're trying to teach me my job!"

"But you don't understand!" repeated Arjan Singh desperately. "Tigers only attack humans because they have to."

"What do you mean they *have to*?!" spluttered the Director wildly, his eyes blazing with fury.

"Tigers don't normally attack humans," said the naturalist. "But humans have wiped out all the tiger's natural prey such as deer and wild pigs. The tiger was starving and there were humans in the forest. The tiger was feeding to stay alive."

"On human flesh," said the Director harshly.

Arjan Singh took a deep breath and tried again.

"Remember, tigers are protected by law. Instead of killing the tiger can't we try another way? Why can't we leave out a few buffalo for it to eat? Then the tiger won't be hungry. And if it's not hungry it won't attack people."

The Director sighed bitterly. "Mr Singh, I'll be frank. If I had my way that tiger of yours would have been dead meat days ago. But my bosses seem to agree with you about not shooting the animal. So I suppose I've got to think your idea over."

But he didn't sound convinced.

A few days passed without a decision from the Director. And meanwhile the tiger struck again. Arjan Singh felt his heart sink as he examined the paw marks.

"Yes, I'm afraid it's the same tiger," he told the wildlife warden who had come with him.

"Well, Mr Singh," said the man grimly. "Looks like the Director will get his way after all. That tiger's a goner now."

A few metres along the path made by the tiger as it dragged its prey, lay a gory human head. It was all that remained of the tiger's latest victim.

Arjan Singh imagined the Park Director's scornful voice. He would say: "I told you so! It's your fault – if I'd had my way that man would still be alive."

The naturalist dreaded the next meeting. Could anything save the tiger now?

What do you think happened next?
a) The Park Director got his way. The tiger was hunted down and shot.
b) Arjan Singh got his way. The Director agreed to put food out for the tiger and it never again attacked people.
c) The tiger was shot with a tranquillizing dart and moved to an area far away from humans.

Answer: b) The Director's bosses still wouldn't allow him to shoot the tiger so he came round to Arjan Singh's idea. The tiger ate the food provided and stopped attacking people. Nowadays many man-eating tigers are moved to areas away from where people live.

Tiger tracker's tips
Here are some more tips to avoid being eaten by a man-eating tiger. (Hopefully there aren't too many around where you live.)
1 A tiger tries to creep up on you from downwind. Always keep an eye out for movements from that direction.
2 A tiger is more likely to attack you if you crouch down.

It thinks you're a four-legged animal rather than a human. So it's a very bad idea to squat down to go to the toilet in the jungle.

3 Tigers attack from behind you. In 1987 people living in the forests on the borders of India and Bangladesh were issued with plastic face masks to wear over the backs of their heads. Tiger attacks virtually stopped because the tigers thought people were looking at them when their backs were turned. It was the next best thing to eyes in the back of their heads.

WHY HAS EVERYONE STARTED RUNNING BACKWARDS?

4 If a tiger's after you and you've left your mask at home, the best thing to do is to climb a tree. Most tigers can't climb trees.

BUT DAD, HOW DO YOU KNOW THERE'S A TIGER AHEAD?

5 Tigers always attack the neck. For a person bitten by a tiger it's all over. The chances of getting away are one in a hundred. Yikes! Now you might think that tigers or the humans that shoot them are the nastiest hunters. But you'd be wrong. Think of beady little eyes.

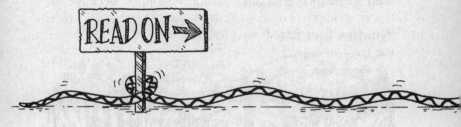

READ ON →

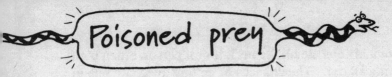
Snakes. Ugh! *They're* nasty enough, but there's a whole army of other horrible hunters that also use poison. Why do they do it? Is it to scare us? Well – no, but it's a very effective way of bumping off smaller creatures. As you're about to find out.

Snakes fact file

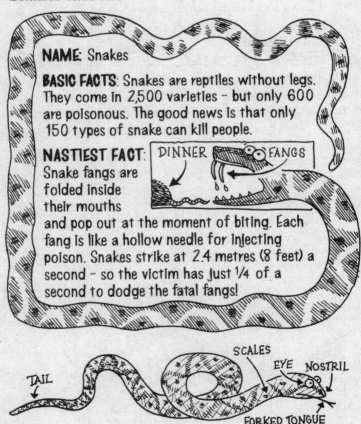

NAME: Snakes

BASIC FACTS: Snakes are reptiles without legs. They come in 2,500 varieties – but only 600 are poisonous. The good news is that only 150 types of snake can kill people.

NASTIEST FACT:
Snake fangs are folded inside their mouths

DINNER   FANGS

and pop out at the moment of biting. Each fang is like a hollow needle for injecting poison. Snakes strike at 2.4 metres (8 feet) a second – so the victim has just ¼ of a second to dodge the fatal fangs!

SCALES

EYE   NOSTRIL

TAIL

FORKED TONGUE

SINISTER SNAKES

NAME: King Cobra

DESCRIPTION: Up to 5.5 metres (18 feet) long.

LIVES: India, southern China and south-east Asia.

FIERCE FEATURES: Has a sinister pattern of two eyes and a nose on the hood behind its head. It displays this when it's angry or scared.

HORRIBLE HABITS: Eats other snakes. (Come to think of it this habit could be quite useful.)

THE BAD NEWS: Its poison is strong enough to kill an elephant. So we humans don't stand a chance.

NAME: Okinawa Habu

DESCRIPTION: Up to 2 metres (6 feet 6 inches) long. Slender body with blotchy yellow ringed markings.

LIVES: Okinawa and neighbouring islands, Pacific Ocean. (Fortunately it doesn't live anywhere else.)

FIERCE FEATURES: Heat-detectors on its head help it to find warm living flesh.

HORRIBLE HABITS: Enjoys snaking into peoples houses through tiny crevices.

THE BAD NEWS: Enjoys biting people.

THE VERY BAD NEWS: It's deadly poisonous.

NAME: Black Mamba

DESCRIPTION: 3-4 metres (10-13 feet) long. Its the largest poisonous snake in Africa.

LIVES: Africa - south of the Sahara Desert.

FIERCE FEATURES: It's said to move as fast as a galloping horse.

HORRIBLE HABITS: It can swallow a whole rat and digest it in 9 hours. Most snakes take more than 24 hours.

Strangely enough, some people like snakes. Indeed, it's an astounding fact that some people even keep snakes as pets! Hopefully, your teacher isn't one of them. Or you might hear facts like these. . .

Five reasons why snakes are cuddly*
* OK, let's just say "not quite so nasty".
1 Snakes are more scared of people than people are of snakes. After all, we're bigger than them.

2 Snakes only bite people if the snake thinks it's being attacked. An Indian tradition says you should stop to chat to a poisonous Russell's viper. That way the snake won't bite you. Talking doesn't help because snakes are deaf (though they can feel sound vibrations passing through the ground). But standing still calms the snake down and could save your life.

226

3 Snakes are useful. Venom from the Russell's viper is made into a medicine that helps blood clot. Malaysian pit viper poison stops blood from clotting and this could be used to prevent unwanted blood clots inside the body.

4 Many nasty snake stories aren't true. For example, the Malaysian pit viper is nicknamed the "hundred pacer" because that's how far people run after being bitten. Then they die. Not true. Victims get at least ten times that distance.

5 Humans kill far more snakes than snakes kill humans. For example, snake blood is used in traditional Chinese medicines. It's said to be very good for your liver and lungs. But not so good for thousands of wretched snakes.

So, fancy a cuddle? Thought not. But if you really find snakes charming why not become a snake charmer? Here's how to. . .

Charm a snake

1 Catch a poisonous snake. A king cobra will do.

2 Remove its venom. Then if things go wrong you won't suffer a fatal bite. This technique is called "milking" the snake. Grasp the snake by the back of its head and make it bite through a piece of paper stuck over a jar. Gently squeeze the poison glands on either side of your snake's head so the lovely poison squirts out. (Don't worry about the snake – it can always make more poison.)

3 Put the snake in a basket and start playing your flute. After a while the snake will stick its head out to take a look.

4 Keep moving your flute about. The snake can't hear the music but it will follow your movements.

5 Beware – it's deciding when to strike!

6 If you get bitten whilst charming a snake and you forgot step 2 it's a good idea to know some First Aid. So here's some useless advice.

Warning: Almost all these remedies are about as useful as a chocolate hot water bottle.

YE OLDE SNAKE-BITE REMEDIES

1 Drink 4.5 litres (1 gallon) of whisky.

2 Cut off your snake-bitten finger with a large knife. Or you could shoot it off with your trusty six-gun. (Traditional cowboy remedy.)

3 Cut the wound open and ask a very good friend to suck out the poison.

4 Soak the bitten hand in paraffin.

5 Wrap chicken meat around the bite. Then burn the meat.

6 Eat a live snake.

7 Squash a toad and squeeze its juices over the wound. (Ancient Roman remedy)

8 Before you get bitten chew some of the snake's poison glands. Or you could make a small wound in your skin and rub in a mixture of spit and poison glands.

Notes

1 This remedy was popular amongst US soldiers in the 1860s. It was even popular with soldiers who hadn't been bitten. In fact, the combined effects of the poison and whisky would probably kill the victim.

2 Useless. By the time the cowboy pulled the trigger the poison would have spread to the rest of his body.

3 This is dangerous because the venom could poison your friend too.

4 Useless

5 Utterly useless – especially for the chicken.

6 Useless and cruel. Snakes have feelings too.

7 Equally cruel and useless.

8 Yes – these do work. They're used by the Kung, San and Zulu peoples of Southern Africa. Anyone for a free trial?

Sensible snake advice

By the way, if someone does get bitten (and there's more chance of winning the lottery) they should remember what the snake looked like. Snake bites are treated with a chemical called an anti-venom. This is a chemical produced naturally by the body in a bid to neutralize the poison. Getting extra amounts injected helps the body to recover more quickly. But the doctors need to know which anti-venom to use. The bite victim should keep very still and send someone for help.

OK – so, snake watching just isn't your favourite pastime. Perhaps a seaside holiday is your idea of fun instead. But just when you thought it was safe to go into the water. . .

Nautical nasties

The most poisonous snakes of all aren't on land. They're in the seas around India and east Asia. Sea-snake poison is *one hundred times* more deadly than any other snake poison. That's the bad news. The good news is sea-snakes don't enjoy biting humans. So Indian fishermen often pull the wriggling snakes from their nets using only their bare hands. Is that brave – or what?

Another nautical nasty is the octopus. Yes – the sinister suckers have a poisonous bite. Scientists aren't sure exactly how poisonous the bite is because no one has volunteered to be bitten. Any takers? It's all in the cause of Science.

Meanwhile, on land things aren't much better. Besides snakes there's a host of other. . .

Pesky poisoners

1 The gila monster has a nasty method of poisoning its prey. This 50 cm-long (19.5 inch) lizard from the southern USA bites its victim. Then it chews the poison into the wound. Ouch!

2 Hot dry regions of the world are home to scorpions. Yes – they like it tough. A scorpion can live without water for three months and live without food for a year. And if it turns chilly – no problem. A scorpion will come back to life after being frozen for a few hours in a lump of ice. (This could be a problem if you tried to make scorpion-flavoured ice-cream.)

3 Scorpions are active at night and hide during the day. Unfortunately, deadly scorpions such as the Trinidad scorpion love to snuggle down in a nice warm shoe. Next morning the shoe's owner gets a nasty surprise. That would really get your day off on the wrong foot.

SPOT THE WOMAN WALKING TO WORK
WITH A SCORPION IN HER SHOE

4 Water shrews are rat-like little beasts. They have poisonous spit that paralyses the frogs and fishes they eat. That way the prey won't try to wriggle free whilst it's being scoffed by the shrew.

5 You've heard of dog eat dog? Well, dog eat toad isn't a very sensible idea either. The toad's warty skin contains glands that make a poison strong enough to kill a dog.

6 Remember the mixed-up duck-billed platypus? Just to confuse you further, the male platypus has poisonous spurs on its ankles. No one knows if the spurs are for fighting off other animals or for stabbing other males in fights over females. I expect they get used on the spur of the moment.

So how do you feel about poisonous creatures now? Worried, anxious, insecure? Join the club. That's what it's like to be a small animal when hungry hunters are on the prowl. Yep – it can be murder out there.

Narrow squeaks

One moment you're nibbling a tasty morsel of smelly cheese. The next, you're running for your life with a hungry monster snapping at your tail. (By the way, the monster's name is Tiddles the cat.) Yes, if you're a mouse, life is full of narrow squeaks.

SORRY ABOUT THIS, IT'S JUST MY NASTY NATURE

Yet amazingly, many creatures manage to get away, or even turn the tables on their attackers. Here's how they do it. . .

Some animals have their very own suits of armour. Could you do with this kind of protection?

MY DOG HAS HIS VERY OWN SUIT OF ARMOUR...

NOT THAT SORT OF ARMOUR – TURN THE PAGE AND YOU MIGHT LEARN SOMETHING!

Nasty Nature Guide To Self Defence

SAFETY FIRST

Stylish armour as worn by the three-banded armadillo of South America. Simply roll in a ball. If you fancy a bit of fun leave a chink in your armour. The attacker will insert a paw into the gap. Then shut the gap like a steel trap. Wham - Crunch - Ouch!

TEACH YOUR ENEMIES A SHARP LESSON

Absolutely foolproof hedgehog and porcupine spiny armour. Choice of defence modes.

Hedgehog: Roll your body in a ball or ram your spines up an attacker's nose. Five thousand spines guaranteed in every hedgehog outfit. *Manufacturer's Warning: Never roll yourself in a ball in front of oncoming lorries. You'll feel a bit flat afterwards.*

Porcupine: Jab your barbed spines into an attacker's body. They won't get them out until their dying day. (That'll be quite soon afterwards.)

FANCY A SWIM?

Don't forget your porcupine fish swimming costume. Just inflate your swimsuit with water and stick your spines out. Gives sharks a real mouthful.

I'M OUT OF HERE!

BE A HERO

With this discreet hero shrew outfit a specially strengthened backbone helps you feel tough inside. Guaranteed – if you're the size of a shrew a fully-grown human can stand on your back and you'll survive.*

NO PROBLEM!

*WARNING
DON'T DO THIS TO YOUR PET HAMSTER. ONLY HERO SHREWS HAVE THIS PROTECTION. OTHER FURRY ANIMALS GET SQUISHED

NO ARMOUR?

So you can't find a suitable suit of armour? No problem. If an attacker gets too close simply kick up a stink. Take some advice from a skunk. If you want to get rid of an attacker try spraying them with foul juices. See next page for details . . .

SKUNK DEFENCE MANUAL

To be carried by all skunks at all times. You never know when you might need it.

1. Always give your attacker a warning. It's only fair to perform this little dance. Try practising it now.

◀ Stamp your feet and arch your back.

▷ Sway your body backwards and forwards.

◀ Stand on your hands and walk on them towards the attacker until you're about 2.5 metres (9 feet) away.

2. If they don't get the message, they're asking for it. Turn your back on the enemy. Raise your tail in the air. Arch your back. Look over your shoulder and check your aim. Ready, steady, FIRE!

3. You're sending a spray that comes from glands on either side of your bottom. Waggle your behind from side-to-side so your enemy gets a good drenching.

Notes

1 The spray contains a chemical called butyl mercaptan (bu-tile mer-cap-tan). It's reckoned to be **the worst smell**

in the world. You can smell it at least 1.6 km (1 mile) away and it stays smelly for over a year.

2 The stink is so horrible that it damages the inside of the nose.

3 The juices taste so disgusting they make the victim throw up.

4 If the spray gets in the victim's eyes it causes temporary blindness.

5 But it doesn't bother us skunks a bit.

The victim shouldn't complain too loudly either, for at least skunk spray isn't poisonous enough to kill. Some animals have really deadly poisonous defences.

Poisonous prey

Sitting on a tin-tack is a mere pin prick. Getting stung by a bee is a sore subject. Jumping in a bed of nettles – that's a little rash. All these things hurt but they're not *really* painful. Nothing like a brush with these creatures. . .

The stonefish uses its poisonous spines in self-defence. The fish lurks in shallow waters around the Australian coast and looks just like a stone (surprise, surprise) buried in the mud. But its poison causes **the worst pain in the world**. Humans who accidentally tread on the spines writhe in agony. Fortunately there's an anti-venom that can save the victim's life.

Don't spit at a spitting cobra. This 2 metres (6 feet 6 inches) long snake is likely to spit back a double jet of fluid from up to 2.5 metres (8 feet). That's bad enough. But the really bad news is the spit is deadly poisonous. One gram (0.035 oz) is enough to kill 165 humans or 160,000 mice. So the last thing on Earth you need is a spitting match with this sinister snake.

In the South American rainforest you'll see happy little frogs hopping about in the trees. "Why are they so brightly coloured?" you wonder. "Perhaps they will want to make friends." No way – they're warning you that they're deadly poisonous. Just 1 gram (0.035 oz) of the poison produced in their skin is enough to kill 100,000 people. Mind you, that doesn't save some frogs from an even worse torture. Amerindians grill the frogs over a fire and tip their arrows with the frog's deadly sweated juices.

So you don't want a frog in your throat? OK – how about a poisonous fish? People with a taste for danger enjoy eating these fish. Honestly – it's true.

SUSHI RESTAURANT MENU

We serve only the finest sushi - the ultimate Japanese delicacy made from delicious raw fish.

TODAY'S SPECIAL: Fugu

Made from the chopped up raw flesh of the puffer fish. You'll be dying to try it!

THE SMALL PRINT.

Warning: This dish is hopefully free of any trace of the poisonous liver, guts, blood and eggs of the puffer fish. Our chefs have trained for three years to cut these bits out. But if you should happen to eat any of these bits you'll die. It won't be our fault, OK? I mean - accidents do happen several times a year.

On the run

If you don't have your own poison, you might try running away. Speedy animals such as antelopes can often out-run a hunter, especially if they've got a head start. The pronghorn – that's a type of antelope from western USA, reaches speeds of 85 km an hour (53 mph); horses and ostriches can gallop at 80 km an hour (50 mph). But how does that compare to us? Well – humans are left gasping. The fastest runners can only run at 36 km per hour (22.5 mph) for short distances. Then they run out of puff.

HURRY UP!

Under cover

If you don't like running, you could stay still and blend in with the scenery. The sloth hangs out in the South American rainforest and moves at a stately 241 metres an hour (0.15 mph). It's so slow-moving that tiny green plants grow on its coat and this colouring makes it hard to spot amongst the trees. The word "sloth" means lazy, and naturalist Charles Waterton objected to the sloth's laid back lifestyle. . .

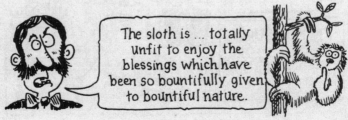

The sloth is ... totally unfit to enjoy the blessings which have been so bountifully given to bountiful nature.

So what's wrong with doing no work and hanging around upside-down in trees?

Many creatures hide successfully because they're the same colour as their surroundings. This trick is called "camouflage". But the real camouflage experts are creatures that change colour to match their surroundings. Take the flounder, for example – that's a type of flat-fish. A scientist once put a chess board on the bottom of a flounder's tank and within minutes the fish was a tasteful check pattern. Small colour grains in the flounder's skin move together or apart in response to signals from its brain. And this colourful trick leaves an attacker . . . floundering.

*PLAICE AND FLOUNDERS BELONG TO THE SAME FAMILY

If you can't change colour, you could try being invisible. Amazingly, some creatures such as the glass cat-fish have see-through bodies. They blend into the background because you can see it through their bodies. Yuck – imagine if you could see your school dinner after you'd eaten it.

Animal acting awards

If all else fails you could pretend to be another more dangerous creature. Preferably something fierce and poisonous or something you wouldn't want to eat. Yes – animals can be actors too. Welcome to the Animal Oscars.

BEST ACTOR/ACTRESS (Snake Category)

RUNNER-UP
The totally harmless king snake almost won for its superb impression of a poisonous coral snake. The king snake has the same red, yellow and black bands on its body but in a different order. So look carefully!

WINNER
The gopher snake wins for an outstanding performance as a rattlesnake. The gopher snake is harmless but hisses like a rattlesnake and even shakes its tail against dry leaves to rattle an attacker's nerves.

BEST ACTOR/ACTRESS (Plant Impression Category)

RUNNER-UP
The tawny frogmouth bird of Australia gives a terrific performance when it's asleep! It always sleeps on a tree branch and looks just like a rotten old twig.

WINNER
The leafy sea-dragon is a sea-horse. It wins this award because it looks just like a disgusting rubbery bit of seaweed.

MOST DISGUSTING MAKE-UP AWARD

RUNNER-UP
The Budgett's frog from Argentina comes second in this category. It can swell up like a big ball of slime and then scream and grunt if you get too close.

WINNER
Our prize winner is the Ecuador tree frog. It sprawls on a leaf and looks just like a disgusting slimy bird dropping.

Strange survival strategies

Animals have plenty more survival tricks and some of them are really strange. Which of these survival strategies is too strange to be true?

1 The horned toad from the western parts of North America squirts blood from its eyes to frighten an attacker. TRUE/FALSE

2 The mimicking macaw of South America warns off attackers with a brilliant impression of an eagle's screech. TRUE/FALSE

3 Pallas's glass snake is actually a legless lizard. (That doesn't mean it's drunk.) When attacked the lizard's 1.5 metre (5 feet) body breaks into wriggling bits. In the confusion the lizard's head end manages to escape. It then grows a new body. TRUE/FALSE

4 *Acanthephyra* (A-can-tha-fi-ra) is a shrimp that lurks in the deep ocean. When attacked it puts on a dazzling display of flashing lights before slipping away into the gloom. TRUE/FALSE

5 The Chilean four-eyed frog has a pair of spots on its thighs that it flashes at would-be attackers. The spots are like a huge pair of eyes and scare most attackers off. TRUE/FALSE

Biting back

Some creatures fight back if their friends are around to give them support. This is surprisingly common and the aim is always to frighten a hunter away. Birds, for example, will attack an owl if there's enough of them around. Chimps will gang up on a leopard and ground squirrels kick sand in a snake's face. Would you dare do this to your local bully?

When an animal is cornered without hope of escape it will often fight for its life. Even mice and their babies do this. So if someone says you're as "brave as a mouse" it's quite a compliment.

And so you reach the end of the day. A day spent dodging horrible hunters and fighting for your life. You're still alive . . . just. Well, congratulations – you must be feeling peckish enough to eat – well, just about anything. I hope so. Now it's time for some gruesome gluttonish guzzling.

Gruesome guzzling

Animals love eating and they always want second helpings. And what's more they don't care about good table manners. Burp! Oh, dear. Look what's coming to dinner. . .

Incredible eating equipment

Every animal has evolved jaws and mouth-parts that are perfectly suited to eating its favourite food. Here are a few examples. . .

1 Giraffes have tongues 30 cm (12 inches) long. Ideal for grasping leaves and yanking them off tall trees. But that's nothing – the South American anteater uses its sticky 60 cm (24 inches) tongue to lick up ants. It can manage as many as 30,000 a day.

2 The Asian and south-east European hamster has floppy cheek pouches to store seeds. It sometimes stuffs these pouches so full that it can scarcely stagger home. These "cheeky" hamsters store as much as 90 kg (200 lbs) of seeds in their burrows.

DINNER → ← LUNCH

BREAKFAST

3 Crocodiles have huge jaws useful for dragging their prey to a watery grave. A one-tonne crocodile has 13 tonnes worth of crushing power in its jaws. That's 26 times stronger than a human bite.

4 Elephants suck water through their trunks. Each trunkful holds 6.8 litres (1.5 gallons) and a thirsty elephant can slurp up 227 litres (50 gallons) at a time.

5 Snake jaws unhinge to allow them to swallow prey that are bigger than their own heads. The African egg-eating snake uses this trick to swallow eggs without breaking them – and they're not even hard-boiled. Don't try this at home.

GO ON DAD, YOU CAN DO IT!

6 If you're a flamingo you eat by turning your head upside-down underwater whilst balancing on your long legs. Tricky. Next you sweep your head from side to side and fill your mouth with water. Then use your tongue and a built-in sieve inside your mouth to suck out little wriggling water creatures. Tasty!

7 Chameleons sit around in trees waiting for insects to drop by. Suddenly a fly buzzes around and the chameleon yawns. Its long sticky tongue shoots out and back before you can see what's happened. The chameleon looks happy – if that's possible – and the fly? It's nowhere to be seen. Frogs and toads feed in the same revolting fashion.

Dare YOU find out for yourself . . . how to drink like a cat?

What you need
Yourself
A bowl of milk or water
A mirror

All you do is
1 Look at your tongue in the mirror. A cat can fold up the sides of its tongue to make a shovel shape. Can you do this?

MUST HAVE RUN OUT OF CLEAN CUPS

2 Try lapping the milk. You then have to flick the milk into the back of your throat with your tongue. How easy is this?
a) No problem at all.
b) It's impossible to get more than a few drops of liquid in your mouth.
c) Totally impossible. Luckily the cat came and drank the milk.

Answer: b) Most humans can't make the right shape with their tongues.

Top tool tricks

If your eating equipment lets you down you could always use tools to help you eat. . .

1 Green jays in the USA hold twigs in their beaks to poke under loose bark to dislodge stray insects.
2 Chimpanzees poke twigs into termite nests and lick the fat, wriggling insects off the twig.
3 A sea-otter breaks open mussels on a stone balanced on its chest as it swims backstroke. (Don't try this in your local pool.)
4Thrushes break open snail shells by banging the molluscs on a stone. You'll find the stones surrounded by broken snail shells.

Apart from the objects they use to help them eat, some animals have. . .

Terrible table manners

1 A toad or frog uses its eyeballs to help it swallow a huge juicy fly. It blinks as it swallows, pushing the eyeballs backwards into its head and lowering the pressure inside the mouth. This makes swallowing easier, even if it looks disgusting. Gulp!

2 The red-billed quela is a small bird that lives in Africa, south of the Sahara desert. Its favourite food is seeds from human crops. Nothing wrong with that, except that the quela likes to fly around in gangs of up to ten million strong. Once that lot have dropped in for dinner there's nothing left for anyone else.

3 Many animals hide spare food. We've all heard of squirrels burying nuts in the autumn, but do you know why dogs bury bones? When they lived in the wild thousands of years ago, dogs buried bones to stop other creatures guzzling the bone marrow. And they're still up to this old trick after all these years. Well – you can't teach an old dog new tricks.

4 The bearded vulture is wild about bone marrow too. The villainous vulture drops bones from a dizzy height of 80 metres (262 feet) on to rocks until they break open. It has been rumoured to do this to unfortunate tortoises as well and even to enjoy dive-bombing mountaineers.

WE'RE RETURNING TO BASE-CAMP. JOHN'S BEEN KNOCKED OUT BY A TORTOISE, OVER...

5 Owls eat small animals whole and then sick up the fur and bones in the form of pellets.

6 Starfish have a stomach-turning method of feeding on rotting fish and other prey. At the vital moment, the starfish squeezes its muscles until its stomach pops out of its mouth. The stomach's digestive juices dissolve the mouldering meal.

7 Many grass-eating animals, such as cows, have a special area of their stomach called the rumen. Here the food is softened for a few hours with stomach juices before being sicked up to the mouth for an extra chew. "Chewing the cud" as it's called, helps to break down the tough plant material so it's easier to digest. Imagine if humans did this. It's certainly something to chew over.

Fundamental food facts

A food chain is nothing to do with clanking chains or dungeons. It's far more fascinating. "Food chain" is a name used by naturalists to describe the vital links between animals and the unfortunate creatures they guzzle. Most food chains start with plants and a typical food chain goes something like this:

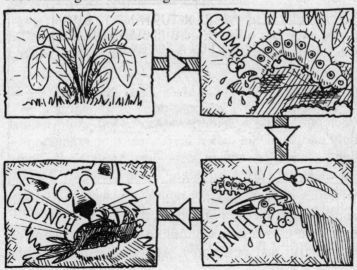

A food web (nothing to do with spiders) links the food chains in a particular habitat. So you might end up with something like this:

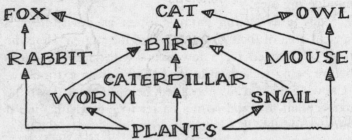

Animals depend on each other and on plants. Take away the plants, and the bugs and rabbits and mice starve. If they disappear the animals that eat them will go hungry too.

Strangely enough if the top animals in the web disappear there can be nasty results too. If the fox died out more rabbits would survive to breed and multiply. Good news for rabbits? Not necessarily. The rampaging rabbits guzzle plants. This is bad news for the bugs, birds, mice and other animals that depend on plants for food and shelter. And of course, the rabbits end up starving too.

Disgusting diets

Each animal has a favourite type of food. Animals that only eat plants are called herbivores (not vegetarians – that's a name for human herbivores). Animals that only eat meat are called carnivores. And creatures that eat both (including humans who enjoy meat and two veg) are called omnivores. Simple, isn't it? But some animals also scoff sickening side dishes. Could you match the animal to the horrible things it eats?

252

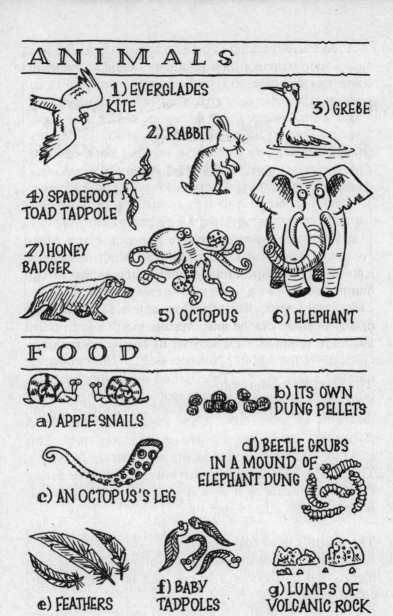

ANIMALS

1) EVERGLADES KITE

2) RABBIT

3) GREBE

4) SPADEFOOT TOAD TADPOLE

7) HONEY BADGER

5) OCTOPUS

6) ELEPHANT

FOOD

a) APPLE SNAILS

b) ITS OWN DUNG PELLETS

c) AN OCTOPUS'S LEG

d) BEETLE GRUBS IN A MOUND OF ELEPHANT DUNG

e) FEATHERS

f) BABY TADPOLES

g) LUMPS OF VOLCANIC ROCK

Answers: 1 a) The kite will only eat snails. So if there aren't any to peck the kite gets peckish instead. **2 b)** Rabbits have a side pocket in their guts filled with bacteria where food rots and becomes easier to digest. By eating its dung the rabbit gives the food a second chance to rot and become more nourishing. Yuck – what a rotten idea. **3 e)** No one knows why they do this, but the feathers may help the bird sick up fish bones. Nice. **4 f)** Yes – its own brothers and sisters. There are two kinds of tadpoles. Harmless little plant eaters and cannibals with sharp teeth. Guess what happens when they get together? **5 c)** An octopus will eat its own leg if it's hungry enough. Luckily for the octopus, it grows another. **6 g)** Elephants visit a cave on Mount Elgon in East Africa to chew chunks of rock. Scientists think the rock contains minerals that keep the elephants healthy. **7 d)** I'd stick to honey!

The world's fussiest eater

Ever had to feed a really fussy pet? This will put your problems in perspective. Cape sugarbirds from South Africa only eat insects that live on the protea shrub. This is a rare plant only found at the southern tip of Africa. This feathered fusspot will also only drink protea nectar. Each bird has its own personal shrubs which it guards jealously from other sugarbirds.

The world's least fussy eater

Like many other birds, ostriches swallow pebbles to help them grind up food in a special part of their stomachs called the gizzard.

Ostriches normally eat leaves and seeds but according

to its owner, one bird ate. . .

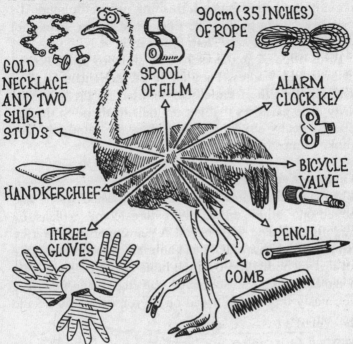

GOLD NECKLACE AND TWO SHIRT STUDS

SPOOL OF FILM

90cm (35 INCHES) OF ROPE

ALARM CLOCK KEY

BICYCLE VALVE

HANDKERCHIEF

THREE GLOVES

COMB

PENCIL

Clean creatures

Dirty animals? Filthy beasts? Don't you believe it! Despite their messy eating habits most animals like to get clean afterwards. But your parents might not approve if you copied some of their washing habits. . .

Cats are supple enough to lick themselves all over. They can even lick their own bottoms – wow! They wash their faces by licking their paws and rubbing their faces. Waste fur sticks to a cat's rough tongue and the front teeth strain out any bits of dirt and dead skin. They sick up any fur they swallow. Like any animal spit, cat spit is good for killing germs in the fur.

African warthogs, hippos, buffaloes and many others like nothing better than a refreshing roll in the mud. It's a sensible thing to do. The thick mud keeps them cool and protects their skin from biting insects.

Birds often clean themselves by allowing ants to crawl all over their bodies. They enjoy the delightful tingling sensation and the formic acid squirted by the ants kills nasty little parasites that get up their feathers. Sitting on top of a really smoky chimney does the same job. The smoke bumps off the pesky parasites.

Nasty scavengers

When an animal has eaten its fill, washed itself, and moved on – a new crowd of creatures comes to feast on the leftovers. The scavengers. A scavenger is a creature that eats food scraps and dead animals. It sounds nasty – but if somebody didn't eat the bones we'd be knee-deep in skeletons by now. So maybe scavengers don't deserve their nasty reputation? Read on, if you dare, and decide for yourself.

Scary scavengers

1 Hagfish (also known as slimefish) look like swimming sausages with no jaws and no bones. They enjoy eating dead fish from the inside out – leaving just the skin and bones.

2 Komodo dragons are huge – they're the largest lizards in the world. These 3-metre (ten-feet) long creatures skulk on the Indonesian island of Komodo. Despite their fearsome appearance, they mainly sniff out dead deer and pigs for their tea.

3 At Harar in Ethiopia until the late 1960s hyenas were used to keep the streets clean of waste meat from butcher's stalls. Each year the hard-working hyenas were rewarded with a lovely smelly dead cow. The hyenas did a good job but they had an embarrassing habit of digging up dead bodies.

4 While we are on this grisly subject, our old friend the snapper turtle (last seen lurking in the sewers) enjoys scoffing unwanted bodies. So keen is the turtle that the police in Florida, USA use tame snapper turtles to sniff out corpses. Imagine what the turtles might get as a treat! And talking about dead bodies. . .

Vultures fact file

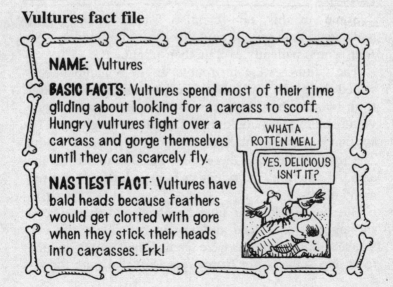

NAME: Vultures

BASIC FACTS: Vultures spend most of their time gliding about looking for a carcass to scoff. Hungry vultures fight over a carcass and gorge themselves until they can scarcely fly.

WHAT A ROTTEN MEAL

YES, DELICIOUS ISN'T IT?

NASTIEST FACT: Vultures have bald heads because feathers would get clotted with gore when they stick their heads into carcasses. Erk!

So would you want to invite a vulture to dinner? Some people would – here's their story.

Vulture restaurants

In 1973 John Ledger, director of the Endangered Wildlife Trust in South Africa was a worried man.

"Poor vultures, we must do something to help them," he said to his friends.

IT'S A REAL PROBLEM

Some of his non-scientist friends didn't quite understand how anyone could feel sorry for a vulture. So John would patiently explain their plight.

The vultures were in trouble. In 1948 mountaineers scaled the peaks of the Magaliesberg mountains not far from Johannesburg and put identification rings on all the vulture chicks they could find. The babies fought back by spitting at the mountaineers – there's gratitude for you. The research showed there were 12,000 vultures in the area. At one time, the scientists believed, there had been many more.

But the district was now farmland and there was a shortage of large dead animals for the vultures to eat. Worse still, the vultures were feeding their young on junk food. No – that's not hamburgers but real *junk* food –

such as ring pulls from drink cans. This diet did nasty things to the vulture chick's insides. Small wonder half the chicks were dying every year.

That's where the vulture restaurants came in. The plan was simple, but brilliant. Fence off an area of land and leave a few carcasses lying around. Make sure you remember to break the bones so the vultures can guzzle the tasty bone marrow. So while some people scoffed at the idea, the vultures scoffed some delicious dead animals.

Today there are more than 100 vulture restaurants offering exciting and varied menus of dead racehorses, bulls and the odd elephant.

And once there was even a human on the menu. Devoted vulture-lover Mickey Lindbergh shot himself in 1987 at a vulture restaurant. His last act on Earth was to make sure his beloved vultures got fed. On his own dead body!

But there's one creature that makes vultures look like innocent little doves. A creature that makes the worst teacher seem tame and rather fluffy. The vile, violent, villainous, verminous, vicious, voracious RAT! Just look what this creature can do:

The adventures of Super Rat

A rat can fall from a five-storey building and land on its feet – *unharmed*.

It can squeeze through a hole the size of a fifty pence coin.

Fight creatures three times its size . . . and win!

A rat can survive being flushed down a toilet. In fact, this could be a new rat water sport.

A rat can fall in the sea and swim for three days without getting tired.

Rats will happily eat soap and drink beer. And scoff anything else remotely edible – including school dinners.

But despite its gross eating habits, a rat can taste tiny amounts of poison in its food. Yes – even if the poison is only one *millionth* of the food's weight.

Rats can gnaw through anything including lead pipes, wood, bricks, concrete and live electrical cables.

Rat teeth grow continuously – if a rat didn't gnaw things its teeth would eventually curl around and pierce its brain!

One fifth of all human food crops are eaten by rats. In India alone the amount of grain eaten by rats would be enough to fill a train 4,800 km (3,000 miles) long.

In return for all this food, rat bites and fleas caught from rats spread at least 20 deadly diseases to humans.

Loveable rats?

Despite all this some people claim that rats aren't so bad. Do you believe them – or do you smell a rat? Here are some nicer rat facts to rattle around in your brain.

1 All this talk about "dirty rats" is very unfair. Rats spend much of their lives licking themselves clean.
2 Rats don't eat humans – when they're alive. So if you're attacked by a rat you can frighten it off by screaming. Well, you would – wouldn't you? That way the rat knows you're still alive and able to fight back.
3 Rats make more affectionate pets than hamsters and guinea pigs. Rats enjoy being stroked and cuddled – but don't try this with wild rats.

4 If you get tired of your pet you could always eat it. Rats taste like rabbit and deep fried rat with coconut oil is a delicious traditional delicacy in the Philippines.

5 One pair of rats can produce up to 15,000 offspring every year. Despite this, rats really care for their families and only eat their babies when they're *really* hungry.

And compared with some animal lifestyles this really is happy families.

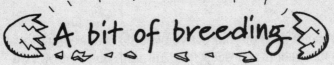

A bit of breeding

What's your family like? Close, friendly, loving? Or do they row a lot and throw things at one another? Many animals care about their young and look after them as best they can. (Tell that to *your* parents.) But some animal families aren't so happy and they have the nasty habit of eating one another. This gives a totally different meaning to the phrase "family meal-times".

Baffling breeding

First stage in setting up an animal family is to find a mate – that's a member of the opposite sex to start a family with. Male animals display a range of baffling behaviour to attract a suitable female.

Just as human teenagers dress up to go out in the evening, male birds "dress up" to attract a mate. Many species grow brightly-coloured feathers, such as the gorgeous peacock or the bottle-green head of a mallard drake.

WHAT A HUNK!

Many male birds sing to attract attention and the females choose the loudest singer. But other animals also "sing" to attract a mate. For example, humpback whales' songs can be heard hundreds of kilometres away – just in case there's a suitable mate in some distant corner of the ocean. Even American grasshopper mice get up on their haunches at mating time and sing squeaky little songs.

Another trick used by some male birds is to build the female a nice cosy nest to lay her eggs in. But no bird goes to the baffling lengths of the bower bird of Australia.

Bird-Brain Estate Agents

HELPING YOU TO FIND YOUR IDEAL NEST

FOR SALE
A beautiful bower

IN BRIEF...
The accommodation consists of a platform with straight walls made of woven plants.

FANTASTIC FEATURES

The bower comes complete with specially chosen designer contents: an interesting collection of blue coloured shells, feathers, bottle tops, pen tops, pegs, animal bones, bird skulls and bits of dead insects. The present owner has painted the walls a tasteful shade of blue using chewed-up blueberries, spit and a stick held in his bill.

Note: 1. Intending purchasers should bear in mind that the property needs repainting every day in any colour so long as it's blue. Also, the neighbouring bower birds often try to steal things from the nest.**

*2. OK, so you don't like blue. Don't worry. Fawn-breasted bower birds only use pale green objects and Lanterbach's bower bird prefer grey and red. So you've a lovely choice of tasteful colour schemes for your nest.

Another method of finding a mate if you're a male animal is to fight off all the other males. This makes the females fancy you and even if they don't you're the only male around. So they don't have any choice.

Male animals that fight include deer (that's why stags grow antlers), cats and giraffes. The giraffes try to butt each other but it generally turns into a neck and neck contest. Male birds also fight. Like most fights between animals of the same species, it's rare for anyone to get killed. Only horrible humans kill their own kind in any numbers. But why then do robins sometimes meet messy ends?

Blood on the tracks

You probably know robins as cute birds that appear on Christmas cards. But have you heard that jolly little rhyme that sometimes gives young children bad dreams?

"Who killed Cock Robin?
I, said the sparrow,
With my bow and arrow,
I killed Cock Robin."

"What a nasty sparrow," you might say. "How cruel to kill such a cute robin." But was the sparrow's confession genuine? Read on and decide for yourself.

THE CASE NOTES OF CHIEF INSPECTOR BIRD

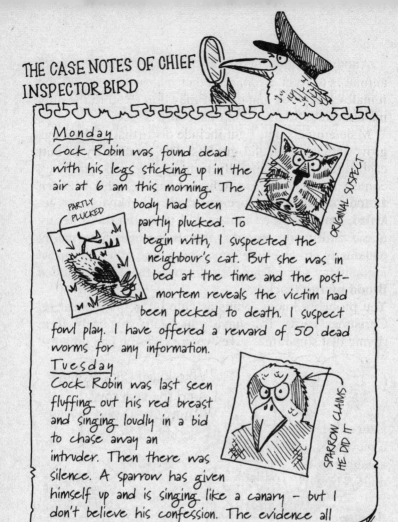

Monday

Cock Robin was found dead with his legs sticking up in the air at 6 am this morning. The body had been partly plucked. To begin with, I suspected the neighbour's cat. But she was in bed at the time and the post-mortem reveals the victim had been pecked to death. I suspect fowl play. I have offered a reward of 50 dead worms for any information.

PARTLY PLUCKED

ORIGINAL SUSPECT

Tuesday

Cock Robin was last seen fluffing out his red breast and singing loudly in a bid to chase away an intruder. Then there was silence. A sparrow has given himself up and is singing like a canary — but I don't believe his confession. The evidence all points in another direction.

SPARROW CLAIMS HE DID IT

Who do you think really killed cock robin?
a) A female robin
b) His own son
c) A passing eagle

Answer: b) Only male robins fight and an eagle would have taken the body to eat. Robins aren't so cute after all. They often fight with their sons over territory because a robin without a territory will starve to death in the winter. Deaths are rare but they do happen.

Dare you find out for yourself . . . how to go to work on an egg?

Some time after mating, female animals give birth. Mammals produce live young but some other groups of animals lay eggs. Dare you discover the secrets hidden inside an egg?

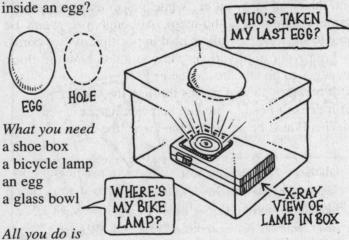

What you need
a shoe box
a bicycle lamp
an egg
a glass bowl

All you do is

1 Draw round the egg on the box lid. Cut a hole just large enough for the egg to lie in without falling through.

2 Put the lamp in the box, switch it on and replace the lid. Place the egg in its hole.

3 Darken the room.

4 You should be able to see the yolk inside the egg.

5 Lightly tap the egg on the side of the bowl and allow its contents to slide into the bowl. Note: That's into the *bowl* and not on the floor.

6 The egg's contents consists of the yellow bit or "yolk" and the clear slimy bit or "white", or to use its scientific name – albumen (al-bu-men). Although you won't be able to see this, the yolk is held in position by two cords.

From your observations can you guess how the chick manages to breathe inside the egg?

a) It breathes air that passes through the shell.

b) It doesn't need to breathe before it hatches.

c) There must be an air bubble inside the egg.

Answer: a) The shell lets in air but not water. The air passes into the developing chick's bloodstream. AND c) An air bubble forms in the blunt end of the egg. Half a mark for this answer because the chick only breathes this air for a few days before it hatches.

Could you be a naturalist?

Most birds feed their young by regurgitating their meals down their chicks' throats. Regurgitation – that's the posh word for being sick, chucking up, etc. Lovely.

Dutch naturalist Nikolaas Tinbergen (1903-1988), tried to discover what triggers this. He noticed that herring gull chicks peck at a red blotch on their parents' beaks. So Tinbergen set out to discover how important this blotch was.

He made a very crude dummy gull's head complete with blotch. He also got hold of a dead gull's head and painted out the blotch. Which did the chicks prefer to peck at?

THE BLOTCH

THEY LOOK UNHAPPY...

...PERHAPS IT'S BECAUSE THEY'VE HAD THEIR HEADS CUT OFF

a) The dead gull's head – they thought it was their supper.
b) The dummy head because it had the blotch.
c) Neither – the sight of the dead gull's head upset the chicks so much they forgot to peck at anything.

Answer: b) What did you expect? Would the sight of a human head make you feel hungry? Tinbergen went on to prove that the red colour wasn't important. Any colour was OK as long as the patch was clearly visible.

Bet you never knew!

Some babies don't look like their parents and their appearance changes completely as they grow up.

1 Tadpoles don't look like adult frogs or toads. Tadpoles have tails and no legs, for example and they have breathing gills outside their bodies. Gradually the gills are absorbed and suddenly a leg or two pops through the tadpole's body. For a while a tadpole might have two or three legs. After all four legs appear the tadpole's tail is absorbed into its body. Life for a frog can be horribly confusing.

2 A baby kangaroo looks like a little pink worm the size of a baked bean. It's only one twelve thousandth the size of its mum.

Somehow it crawls through its mum's fur until it finds her pouch and there feeds off her milk.

After seven months the baby kangaroo, or joey, is big enough to hop around outside the pouch. And after eleven months it has to leave the pouch for good.

Almost immediately another baby takes its place.

3 In terms of growing that's nothing. A blue whale begins its life as an egg produced by its mum that weighs only 0.0009922g (0.000035 oz). The baby blue whale grows to 26 tonnes. That's like you increasing your weight 30,000,000,000 (thirty billion) times.

I HOPE YOU'VE DONE YOUR HOMEWORK, OR THERE'LL BE BIG TROUBLE

Good parents awards

Many animal parents feed and lick their babies clean. And here are some especially good parents. . .

Third prize
Ma Croc
Crocodile mums bury their eggs in the sand by rivers. Ninety-five days later they hear the babies cheeping from inside their eggs and dig them up again. After the babies hatch, mum carries them in her massive jaws down the river and lets them go. For the next few months she feeds them on choice morsels such as juicy frogs, bits of fish and the occasional crunchy insect.

Second prize
Mrs Surinam Toad
She's really ugly – even by toad standards. (Even her friends would agree – if she had any.) She has no eyes,

no teeth and no tongue and a huge mouth that eats anything that moves. Yet somehow she loads her tadpoles on to her back and encases them in bubbles under her skin. Then she patiently carries the tadpoles for two months until they emerge as ugly little versions of herself.

First prize
Mr Emperor Penguin

When Mrs Penguin goes down to the sea to hunt fish, Mr Penguin joins thousands of other males standing about in the freezing cold of Antarctica. Each male balances a single large egg on top of his feet to keep it warm. If the egg falls the chick inside will die. And there the male stands for 40 days and nights without food or shelter until his mate returns. Sometimes the temperatures drops to -40°C (-40°F) What a hero!

Awful animal families

Of course, not all animal families are as caring as that. Many kinds of fish, reptiles and amphibians simply abandon their eggs and leave the young to survive on their own. If they can.

For fish especially, it doesn't matter if some youngsters get eaten. A single cod will lay eight million eggs at a time. If all of them survived the seas would be crammed with cod. And that's what Darwin's idea of natural selection was about. Enough cod will live to breed the next generation.

Not all animals are looked after by both parents. Elephant families, for example, are made up of females under the command of the oldest female. She decides where they go and when they should go for water. The babies are looked after by all the females but when the males grow up they're chased away to live with other males. If you've got an awful brother you might think the elephants have the right idea. If you're a female yourself, that is.

Lethal lessons

If you're a baby animal you need to learn some urgent lessons in survival. And if you're lucky your parents will teach you.

1 Guillemot chicks have to learn how to swim and fly. So their parents chuck them off a cliff. If they fly – good. If not, they'd better learn to swim.

2 Mother swallows take food to their chicks but hover just out of reach. If the chicks want to grab their grub they'd better learn to fly first.

3 Cheetah mums catch a gazelle and then release it for their cubs to chase. If the gazelle escapes the cubs get taught a lesson: they starve.

4 Eventually, when her cubs get too big, a grizzly bear mum chases them up a tree and wanders off. Now begins the biggest lesson of all: how to survive alone.

But every young animal (and human children too) must learn one other lesson. At the end of the day they'll need to go to sleep. But while you're tucked up in your bed some creatures are on the prowl. And they're out to make a killing.

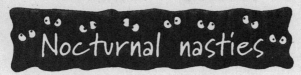

Night. A time of mystery and . . . danger. It's hard to see in the dark and things appear strange and sinister in the moonlight. There are sudden sounds – a scream or is it just a squawk? Something scuttles through the undergrowth. And in the shadows something dark and menacing is looking for its first meal of the night. Will you live to see the dawn?

Nocturnal (that means active by night) animals are adapted to living at night. Their bodies have evolved to suit their lifestyle in certain ways.

Take an African bushbaby, for example. This cute monkey-like creature lives in trees. It spends the night hunting insects, birds, fruit and anything else it can grab.

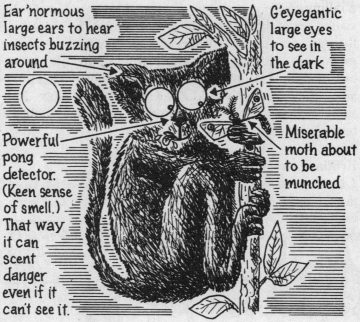

Ear'normous large ears to hear insects buzzing around

G'eyegantic large eyes to see in the dark

Powerful pong detector. (Keen sense of smell.) That way it can scent danger even if it can't see it.

Miserable moth about to be munched

You might think that being nocturnal sounds rather tiring. But consider the advantages for a small animal. It's cool and moist at night which is fine if you live in a hot, dry country. There are lots of shadows to hide in and many of the larger, fiercer creatures are fast asleep.

Unfortunately, there are nocturnal hunters too. Owls swoop out of the darkness to grab unsuspecting shrews in their grasping talons. Hyenas and lions prowl the African grasslands and bats screech through the skies. Have you ever seen bats flapping around in the evening? Creepy – aren't they? And you wouldn't want to get too close. But some naturalists are batty about bats. According to them bats are brilliant. Here's why. . .

Brilliant bats

1 Bats spend ⁵⁄₆ of their lives hanging upside-down from the ceiling. According to a bat scientist, that's an interesting way to live.

AND I SHOULD KNOW!

2 Baby bats are born upside down. Usually their mother catches them before they hit the ground and they cling to their mother's fur with their teeth. Could you imagine a human baby doing this?

NURSE! CATCH MY BABY!

3 You can't say "blind as a bat" because bats aren't actually blind – although they can't see well. But then bats don't need eyes. As they fly, they make high-pitched calls and listen for echoes bouncing off the body of a flying insect. By homing in on these echoes a bat can gobble up a nice juicy insect in mid-air.

4 A bat can make 200 calls a second. Every time it calls, it switches off its hearing to avoid being deafened. Otherwise people would say it's "as deaf as a bat".

Could you be a naturalist?

Naturalist Merlin D. Tuttle set up a series of bat experiments in the early 1980s. He wanted to study how bats hunt the frogs that lived in a muddy bug-infested pond in Panama. He was helped by fellow naturalist, Michael Ryan, who was studying frog mating behaviour. Can you predict the results of their tests?

Experiment 1

Could the bats tell which frogs were edible and which were poisonous? The scientists placed a bat in a cage large enough to fly around in. Then they played tapes of edible and poisonous frogs croaking. What happened?

a) The bat attacked the tape recorder whenever it heard a frog croaking.

b) The bat only dive-bombed the tape recorder when it heard the edible frog.

c) The bat attacked the scientists. This didn't answer the question but it did prove that bats will attack anything that moves.

Experiment 2

Next they tested the frogs. Could they see the bats coming to get them? The scientist made a model bat and ran it along a wire above the frogs' pond. What did the frogs do?

a) They couldn't see the model and carried on croaking.

b) They could see the model and croaked even louder to scare the bat away.

c) They went deadly quiet when the model flew over.

Experiment 3

Do bats recognize frogs by their shape or by sound? Tuttle held a silent frog in one hand and rubbed the fingers of his other hand together to make a swishing sound. Did a bat attack the frog or the naturalist's fingers?

a) The fingers and Tuttle got a nasty nip.

b) The frog

c) Neither, it got tangled in his hair. This proves the bats were bewildered by this sound.

> **Bet you never knew!**
> Carlsbad cavern, New Mexico, USA is alive with bats. Up to twenty million Mexican free-tailed bats go there each summer. The babies hanging from its walls are packed together 2,000 to a square metre (1.2 square yards). But somehow mother bats, returning from a night's hunting, find their own babies using hearing and smell. They recognize the babies in the crowd by their cries and the smell of their bodies. And naturalists have found that the bats are right 80 per cent of the time.

Nasty sleeping habits

Most animals don't bother to go out at night. They like nothing better than a good night's kip. Many naturalists believe that animals and humans sleep because they've nothing better to do. They can't see in the dark and they've eaten during the day. So why not have a little rest? Mind you, some creatures have nasty sleeping habits.

1 Chimps construct beds from springy branches. But they don't bother to make their beds in the morning.

They simply throw them away together with any dirt and fleas. Don't you wish you could do this?

2 When parrot fish go to sleep they wrap themselves in a ball of slime with a small hole to breathe through. This keeps them safe from marauding eels.

3 Only birds and mammals dream. Fish, amphibia and reptiles don't.

4 The prize for the most uncomfortable sleeping position must go to the blue crowned hanging parrot. This bird sleeps hanging upside down from a branch. Its green back looks like a leaf so there's less chance of being spotted by a hunter.

Some animals find it pays to be asleep most of the time. Take the Australian koala, for example.

A DAY IN THE LIFE OF A KOALA

The night

Clambered about in my tree.

Guzzled 1kg (2lbs) of eucalyptus leaves – this is the life. Yawn. Now for a bit of shut-eye – reckon I've earned it.

> **NOTES:** Koalas are more active at night. The disgusting taste of leathery eucalyptus leaves doesn't bother them at all.

5.10am

Found a nice branch to curl up on. Zzzzzz.

> **NOTES:** The koala's diet of leaves isn't nourishing. In fact, it sends them to sleep!

7.30am

Some human woke me up! Can't they let a koala have a decent kip? They've slung a rope loop around my neck.

What cheek! Now they're trying to yank me off my tree – better dig my claws in.

> **NOTES:** When there are too many koalas in an area it's a good idea to move some before they eat all the eucalyptus leaves and starve. Not all koalas like their new homes, however. Some homesick koalas have made their slow way back to their favourite tree!

7.32am
Arggggh! They've caught me. Lucky I've got sharp claws and teeth. Grrr! That will teach them a lesson.

10am
I've been moved in a crate. Oh well – this tree looks OK. Back to sleep.

ZZZ

5, 6, 7 pm
Zzzzz

9pm
Yawn. What's for breakfast. Eucalyptus leaves will do just fine.

284

Winter slumberland

Many animals don't stop at sleeping the night away. Some sleep most of the winter and only get really active in the spring. This is called hibernation – but you probably know that already. So here are a few more details to keep you awake.

Hibernation is a good idea because animals need lots of food to keep warm in cold weather. But during the winter there is less food around. By sleeping much of the time an animal can survive without having to find this extra food. Some animals live off stored food in their burrows and others live off their own body fat – built up by guzzling as much as possible in the warmer months.

Animals that hibernate include tortoises, squirrels, dormice, bats and some snakes. During hibernation an animal's breathing and pulse slow down and its body temperature may drop by 50°C (112°F). It's in a very deep sleep and it can appear dead. This has led to early burials for many unfortunate tortoises.

Zzzzz.

POOR OLD FLASH, HE WAS A LOVELY TORTOISE

PITY I DON'T SNORE – AT LEAST THEY'D HAVE KNOWN I WAS STILL ALIVE

Nasty nature?

Some animals seem really nasty. They look repulsive and do nasty things to other animals. Some animals have horrible weapons or use nasty cunning tricks to catch their prey. Some eat really foul food. And their eating habits are enough to put you off your dinner.

BUT IT'S MY TURN TO PECK THE EYEBALLS OUT

But so what? You can't expect animals to be polite and kind to one another. These are qualities you might find in humans – if you're lucky. Animals have to be tough to survive in a tough world. For them it's more important to be alive than to be nice. For an animal, every day is a battle for life. Animals don't know when they wake up in the morning whether they'll see the day through, or end up as a tasty snack for a larger creature.

WHERE'S FRED?

And for all their nasty habits, we humans find animals immensely useful. They provide the raw materials for our food, and horses and dogs work hard for us. Unlike some humans – animals are *never* boring. We laugh at them and enjoy their companionship. Of course, some animals are nasty but they're also beautiful, fascinating and splendid in their dazzling variety.

You can see why naturalists spend their entire lives studying animals in their natural habitats. And how they get horribly excited if they manage to photograph a rare creature from an unusual angle. Yep, there's no doubt – for us humans, animals have a nasty fascination. But that's Horrible Science for you!

HORRIBLE SCIENCE

Science with the squishy bits left in!

Ugly Bugs
Blood, Bones and Body Bits
Nasty Nature
Chemical Chaos
Fatal Forces
Sounds Dreadful
Evolve or Die
Vicious Veg
Disgusting Digestion
Bulging Brains
Frightening Light
Shocking Electricity
Deadly Diseases
Microscopic Monsters
Killer Energy
The Body Owner's Handbook
The Terrible Truth About Time
Space, Stars and Slimy Aliens
Painful Poison
The Fearsome Fight For Flight
Angry Animals

Specials
Suffering Scientists
Explosive Experiments
The Awfully Big Quiz Book
Really Rotten Experiments

Two horrible books in one
Ugly Bugs and Nasty Nature
Blood, Bones and Body Bits and Chemical Chaos
Frightening Light and Sounds Dreadful
Bulging Brains and Disgusting Digestion
Microscopic Monsters and Deadly Diseases

Large-format colour hardback
The Stunning Science of Everything